D.A. Bennett began writing poetry and short stories during high school years continuing through college. Born into a military family, D.A. moved frequently, 23 times in 26 years. His life experience from family and his own military service provided a desire to explore life from Newfound and to his summers in Louisiana. His adventures awaited until writing and story-telling became a passion. All that he has written is honest and truthful except what purposefully is not.

Enjoy this read, you just might wish you had been there with him.

To my wife Gayle, my mother Doris, aunt Robbye, Bob-o Jack, Samantha, Christy, Mackenzie, Jason and Bryan.

LIFE IS A STORY

by

D.A. Bennett

AUSTIN MACAULEY PUBLISHERS™

LONDON • CAMBRIDGE • NEW YORK • SHARJAH

Ordering Information
Quantity sales: Special discounts are available on quantity purchases by corporations, associations, and others. For details, contact the publisher at the address below.

Publisher's Cataloging-in-Publication data
Bennett, D.A.
Life is a Story

ISBN 9798886933321 (Paperback)
ISBN 9798886933338 (ePub e-book)

Library of Congress Control Number: 2023918105

www.austinmacauley.com/us

First Published 2024
Austin Macauley Publishers LLC
40 Wall Street, 33rd Floor, Suite 3302
New York, NY 10005
USA

mail-usa@austinmacauley.com
+1 (646) 5125767

Deepest appreciation for supported assistance Roxanne
Tankard Raynon, Nancy King, Gayle Bennett.
David Saylock.

Table of Contents

CLYDE

Eva lifted the headphones off her ears and slid them over the bun tying the back of her hair. She carefully placed the headset on the counter in front of the plugs on the new telephone switchboard. Wires were pulled up and placed in the correct slots to connect one callers telephone to the receiving telephone.

At first, the new system was very confusing, but Eva soon learned the peculiar workings of the board and could recognize all the calls and answers of those lucky enough to afford the newest modern 'talky thing' device.

What startled Eva at 5:30 this early morning was someone singing outside the small two-story building that housed the new-fangled telephone exchange. Slowly, she got up from her chair walked to the window and peered out to the street lit only by a single street light.

She could see her brother-in-law, Clyde, meandering down the street, carrying what looked like a pint bottle of whiskey in his hand and singing, 'Give Ireland back to the Irish'. More of a shout than a song. He started walking in the open field toward the wooden grandstands of the town's pride – an actual wooden baseball stadium.

It had multilevel wooden seats with a large wooden and chicken wire back stop. Fencing surrounded much of the open land in the middle of the small town of Greenwood.

Baseball was the lifeblood of most of the Irish immigrants who populated Greenwood, and any man worth his salt played the rough and tumble baseball common to other back wood towns in south Louisiana.

The Greenwood Foxes were the toughest and most despised team in the backwoods league. They played rough spikes high slides type of ball. Stealing bases and dangerously high inside pitches were their specialty. But they had been in first place come the end of the season for the previous three years.

Eva turned and hurried back to the telephone switchboard, reached for a connecting wire, plugged it in and quickly dialed a number on the rotary dial.

Norma Fitzhugh was frying bread for an early morning breakfast before leaving for work. She had a short drive in her old Plymouth to the Angola Penitentiary for the criminally mental ill in Angola, Louisiana. She was in a hurry, not wanting to be late.

Good State jobs were hard to come by and Clyde was out of work again and they needed her paycheck.

Norma heard the telephone ring twice, which meant the call was for the Big House where she and Clyde lived. The house was the original family home built in 1900 where 11 children had been born and raised.

All of the original 11 children were grown and moved out of the parish to Baton Rouge or to the oil fields of Lake Charles. Some left their home town and state never to return.

However, Clyde met Norma and knew each other for only six months when both realized they were passionately in love. Norma knew that Clyde would be a rough one to handle but his passion, determination and good looks were too much for her. Both were madly in love so they married in a simple wedding held at the Big House.

After a brief but loving honeymoon in Baton Rouge, they both wanted to live in Greenwood. Big Papa and big Mama, Clyde's parents, had passed and none of the brothers and sisters wanted to move back to the small town. It was obvious to all the family that Clyde and Norma both loved the slow-moving, easy-going town and they would forever call their home.

By staying, Clyde and Norma inherited the house. It needed some fixing up but Clyde vowed he 'wasn't never leaving till they carried his body out the front door'.

Hearing the telephone ringing, Norma ran down the long hallway of the house to the wooden telephone box hanging on the wall. It seemed to her like modern conveniences were changing and coming fast. She had decided that she needed a way to keep in touch with the office in Angola.

So, she had bought 'the damn thing' and had it installed. She answered in her clipped southern drawl, "Mornin', Eva. What's got you a stirring this time of the day?"

Her sister-in-law, Eva, nervously said, "Clyde's a walkin' cross the ball field headed toward the house, and I think he's purty durn drunk singin' loud enough to wake the dead."

"Well," said Norma, "what the hell is he singin' now?"

Eva reached over, pushed the window up and said, "Now he's a yellin' 'bout goin' down to the Monteleone."

"Jesus, Joseph and Mary, if he ain't lost his damn mind. What the hell am I gonna do with his no-count ass?" Norma pleaded.

"Well," Eva said, "you best figure it out quick, cuz he's on his merry-singing way. Oh God, he just finished off his bottle and threw it at the back stop on the ball field."

Norma replied, "Well, he thinks he just struck out Mickey Mantle. I'll get him calmed. Thanks for callin', Eva. You best watch Son. You know how them two are when they get the drink."

Eva sighed, "Lordy, Lordy, Norma. How we stayed with them two, I'll never know." Son was Clyde's older brother by two years. And both women knew when their husbands got together, all hell could break lose.

But Clyde meant no real harm with his antics. He'd been over to Jackson Landing at Luke Faucheaux's juke joint having a drink or two with the Stanley brothers. As usual, things got to ripping.

Then, the friendly but drunken arguments started, and they were all out in front by the railroad lines that carried logs to the surrounding saw mills. Clyde was in a boisterous mood so he challenged each brother to wrestle. As usual, the winner would be the Louisiana wrestling champion, at least for the night.

Of course, a challenge made was a challenge taken. Each man took a turn trying to flip or trip one or the other. Clyde, as usual, won the so called 'Louisiana championship', and Mr. Faucheaux awarded the winner a pint of Old Overholt bourbon, commonly referred to as Old Overshoes, but still drinkable.

Clyde would normally down a pint in two long drinks, but he'd saved this one for the trip home. He hitched a ride to Greenwood with Ned Stanley, Clyde's sister's husband, whose career was occasional work but plenty of fishing, fighting and fidlin' around.

After continuing their friendly argument, Ned dropped Clyde off at the old Esso station on the main road leading into to town and told him to walk home.

The early morning sun was a colorful orange glow in the crimson blue eastern sky. Clyde was feeling little pain after a night of drink but thought what a lucky man he was to live quietly with great friends and a wonderful understanding wife.

Yet as he strolled across the big field where the battered wooden baseball stadium was standing, he thought and longed for his younger days and good times. He laughed out loud as he remembered an incident at the ole Esso gas station that occurred sometime around thirty years ago.

The incident, as he recalled it in his alcohol altered brain, started when Clyde and his brother, James, known to all as Son, were hanging around the Esso station and general store on a slow Friday evening. Son was busy with his pocket knife whittling away at a piece of wood.

A cool October breeze was gently blowing as a man, stunningly dressed in a fine suit sporting a tweed Irish flat cap, walked toward Clyde and Son.

He stood about five feet away, staring at both then spoke up asking, "Say could you fine looking fellows help me with a tire problem?"

Son looked up from whittling and said, "What kinda tire problem?"

"Well," the man replied with a huge smile, "the kind where the damn thing won't roll."

Clyde, Son and the man all burst out laughing at the same time. The man said he'd make it worth their while. "I'll give you $5 bucks a piece for your effort and $10 each if you're good company."

They laughed then looked at each other as Clyde asked, "Where's the car?"

The man replied, "Oh, about a half-a-mile north of here."

They both sized the man and looked at each other and Clyde said, "Why sure, we be glad to help."

They followed him to his car, chatting friendly along the way. After the brief walk, they saw the car, the likes of which they'd never seen before and would most likely never see again. It was a big, beige Auburn roadster with brown leather interior. It was a fast and beautiful car that screamed, "I'm rich and you're not."

Son said, "Now that is one fine looking automobile."

Looking at Clyde, Son said with a big smile, "Now don't you scratch this man's dreamboat."

Clyde said, "Not on your life. Now let's get to work. This gentleman's obviously anxious to get some place better than Greenwood."

The two brothers got busy on the tire changing while the man stood by telling jokes, talking and smoking a cigarette. He offered a cigarette and Son took him up saying, "One hell of a smoke."

The man said, "Here keep the whole pack."

Son gave a big smile and said, "I'll trade you handing the man his bag of Bull Durham."

The man said, "Why that's a fair trade. I like you gentlemen."

The talking meandered around until the man asked Clyde and Son, "Either of you young gentlemen know how to get to Ms. Boudreaux's whore house?"

They both began to laugh, and Son said, "Why, Mister, you got a long drive cause Ms. Boudreaux's house is in New Orleans."

The man laughed and replied, "Hell, boys, I know that. I just figured two fine young gentlemen like yourselves might know where it's located in New Orleans."

They all laughed together. "Ain't never been there but when you find it, let us know," Clyde croaked through his laugh.

They each told old stories about New Orleans and chewed the fat a little more about the finer parts of the Big Easy life when Clyde asked, "Where you staying when you get there if not at Ms. Boudreaux's?"

The man replied with a big smile, "Why, boys, there's only one place to stay if not at Ms. Boudreaux's fine establishment and that's the Monteleone Hotel."

Clyde smiled and said, "I'll remember that next time I'm down that way."

Finally, the tire was fixed and put back on the roadster. The man finished his smoke and gave each a $10-dollar bill, which was big money anywhere during the Great Depression, especially in backwater Louisiana. He stuck out his hand and said, "Great meeting you fellas. Gable is my name, **Clark Gable**."

Clyde and Son both shook his hand and introduced themselves and told the man how much they appreciated the work. Told him if he was ever up this way to stop in for a quick snort and a smoke. With a big smile, Gable replied, "You got a deal, and I'm buying whatever you boys are drinking."

The story stayed around for years. It got better every time either one told it. Each time the story was told Clyde would quickly add, "If ol' Clark had a offered me a ride, I'd have jumped right in and headed to Noleans. Seafood gumbo, Jax beer and Ms. Boudreaux's fine establishment."

Of course, he always said this when Norma was nowhere to be found.

Clyde continued his trek across the ball field laughing and singing until he finally reached the Big House. Standing in the local street, he stood in the morning light thinking 'home'.

Norma stood at the door with a broomstick in her hand watching him make a damn fool of himself. She walked down the steps with the determined look of hurt on her face. Opening the gate, she whacked Clyde hard on his shoulder with the stick.

Although, she'd been aiming at his head, she was glad she'd missed, or she'd have knocked him out. He howled with pain and indignation as he tried to stand.

Carefully, he got to his feet, keeping a close eye on Norma and her stick. His shirt and arm were both torn and blood flowed from his arm over his good work shirt.

"Damnit, Norma, why'd you whack the livin' hell out of me?" He yelped in pain.

"Cuz you swore you'd stop your durn drinkin'. You promised no more comin' home at 5:00 in the morning smellin' like some damn juke joint. What the hell am I supposed to do with you?"

"And now you've done ruined your best shirt. Damn you, Clyde, just to hell and back damn you," she hollered, all the while shaking the broomstick at him.

"Aw, sweetheart, you know I love you more than anything or anyone in this old world. I just got caught up in the cahoots of them Stanley boys, and I had to whoop both of em. Luke Faucheaux said the winner would get a pint, and he gave me the bottle as my reward for whippin' 'em one at a time. Hell I think I even whooped both at the same time," Clyde laughed still numbingly drunk.

Norma gave a small smirkish grin and reproached scowlingly, "Listen here, Clyde, get your Black Irish ass into the house, get some coffee into you and sober up so I can get to work. You best be quick with it and find yourself work today cause I'm carrying your ass, and I'm damned tired."

Clyde knew he was in serious trouble. No messin' with her now cuz when Norma gave him her sly grin, it weren't no laughing-type grin; it was her 'get going or get out cause I'm the boss' grin. Clyde climbed the stairs and opened the screen door, careful to let Norma pass through first. "Ladies afore gentlemen," he said timidly.

Norma replied, "I ain't seen no gentlemen round these parts in a coon's ass age. Now get that coffee in you and get your drunk self-sober and to movin'."

Clyde walked slowly down the hallway lit by bare light bulbs hanging from the ceiling. He carefully made his way to the kitchen where he reached to the open shelf cabinet and pulled a mug for his coffee. Looking around he found and reached for the white French drip pot that was already sitting in a pan of hot water on the back of Norma's new electric stove.

The coffee came out hot and strong. He took a big swallow and savored the chickory flavor even as it scalded his tongue. The coffee quickly popped his head into a short, but reasonable, sober state of mind. Clyde said to no one in particular, "Durn good coffee, sweetheart."

Norma heard him and scolded, "Don't you be 'sweethearting' me. Get cleaned up, get some clothes on, get down to the state highway barn and see if you can get some work. So, get to getting instead of getting to nothing."

"You know that ol fool Woodrow Summerton; he's always looking for equipment operators. You best get yourself together and get moving. I've got to be at work in 30 minutes. Bye-bye."

She leaned down and kissed his forehead. He held her close and said, "Honeybunch, I love you more every moment I live."

Norma replied, "Then go get a damn job."

After he heard the front screen door slam and Norma's old Plymouth go speeding off to her eight-hour day, Clyde pushed his chair back slowly. Getting up from the kitchen table, he made his way to the screen door onto the back porch and the water well.

The water well was the center of country living. Water, the backbone of life. Firmly standing lonely on the broken-down porch the well represented a family history in a slow but subtle decline.

He carefully lowered the galvanized metal bucket down the well until the bucket hit water. Lowering it until it felt full, he pulled the rope through the top-end pulley until the bucket appeared at the narrow opening. Stretching his arm to reach the bottom of the bucket, he poured water into the white enamel bowl on a wooden plank shelf.

He tied the bucket of remaining water to two 10-penny nails hammered into the 4x4 post that supported the metal roof covering the porch.

Stripping off his shirt, he appeared to be painted white and brown. Some called it a farmer's tan, but it was more like a workman's tan – a white chest and back and tanned brown arms, neck and face. His body was that of a hard-boned and hard-working Irish man.

He had a few nasty scars – one on the right shoulder from a missed knife stab that sheared off part of his right breast; there were others here and there from hard work as a railroad fireman on the long-forgotten, coal-fired steam engines.

His cheeks and chin were bone hard, yet a good-looking man with pale blue eyes, jet-black hair cut short and short on the sides with a long thick black streak running from front to back. From the cut of him, it was obvious to most that he was definitely a man to be reckoned with, and a man you would want by your side when trouble started.

He bent down and splashed water on his face. The water was clean and refreshing, while the clean towel, hanging on the nails, was rough and brisk. He wiped under his arms and splashed more water on his body and wiped hard with the rough towel.

Deciding he best shave, he lathered up the shaving cup and quickly brushed the soap on his face. Looking into the small, round mirror hanging on the 4x4, he began to pull the new Gillette double-blade razor that Norma bought him across his face. The shave was smooth, easy and quick.

He finished, wiped off the remaining lather and looked for nicks of blood, only a few and the styptic pencil would fix those. He patted his face with Old Spice as he softly sang a verse from the Hank Williams' song, 'Hey, good looking'.

Then his longing thirst returned. He walked down the steps of the back porch out to the fox hound pen. The hounds howled and barked, anticipating their morning feed. But the hounds would have to wait as Clyde carefully lifted a log and pulled out a bottle of Old Granddad bourbon. He took a big drink and put the cap back on and hid the bottle.

He then went to the back of the dog shed and picked up a 50 pound bag of Purina dog chow and slowly poured the food evenly into the long feeding trough, allowing each of the nine hounds a chance at the morning feed.

Picking up a large can of bacon fat, he added that to the trough, and the ravenous hounds ate and snapped at each other until they finally settled and ate every morsel.

A quick stop at the outhouse and then at 7:30am, it was time for his favorite show. He walked back up the porch, sat down in his old metal rocker, positioned to provide a great view of the sun coming up and the stirrings going on at Son and Eva's house, not more than a hundred yards south. Perfect light, interesting sight.

Each morning at precisely 7:30, Clyde's older brother, Son, would come out on his back porch and go through his morning ritual shave. Clyde would anxiously watch each move that Son made and talk to himself, explaining in great detail Son's morning shaving habits.

Brush by brush, stroke by stroke, Clyde would sit back, watch and laugh out loud until Son would finally look up see him, then hold his taught right arm and give Clyde his middle 'screw you' finger. Clyde would roar with laughter.

This little show and response had gone on for years. How strange the memories he thought about their foolish past. But Clyde or Son never said a word about their early-morning antics. Their game was between two Irish brothers and the secret of respect, love of life and humor only they could share.

After his morning ritual with Son, Clyde decided it was time to get moving or else Norma would have his hide hung on the outhouse wall. She always made a call to the State Highway Barn to see if he had shown up looking for work.

It was ready-made work for Clyde because he was considered one of the best road-equipment operators in the parish, if not the state.

He stood and slowly lowered the galvanized well bucket again until it touched water in the well then slowly raised the filled bucket and balanced it on the porch. He quickly stripped off all of his clothes and jumped down off the porch and stood naked as the world had brought him.

He raised the bucket above his head and poured the ice-cold water over his body. Reaching for a bar of Ivory soap, he quickly lathered up from head to toe. As part of the ongoing 'messin' with Son', he bent down with his rear end facing Son's house to wash his feet. Seeing the moon, Son yelled, "No need to show it, Clyde, everyone knows you're the biggest ass in all Louisiana."

Clyde again had a hardy laugh as he rinsed off and reached for his towel quickly drying off. Slipping back into his pants, he walked up the porch steps and into the bedroom where he opened his cedar closet and got a new starched green work shirt. Quickly gathering his knife, lucky stone and wallet, he walked to the front door.

No need to lock it, he thought, *ain't no one got the balls to mess with the Fitzhugh Big House.*

He slid into the front seat of his new Buick Skylark – small car with a big V-8 and 3-speed on the column. No frills just a hot little car. He cranked the driver's side window down then started the V-8.

He gunned the engine a couple of times then popped the clutch and shot up the gravel parking spot in front of the Big House as he hit the gas pedal hard.

He was heading south to the State Highway Barn at a crisp 75 mph arriving at 8:30, just as the other workman were heading to their job sites.

Clyde turned off the highway and into the department's heavy equipment area. He parked got out of the car, slammed the door hard for good measure and walked straight and tall into the main office.

The road boss, Woodrow Summerton, sat behind his desk smoking the first of his 10 cigar daily habit.

"So, the great Clyde Fitzhugh shows his shiny white ass looking for work no doubt?" Woodrow said through a puff of smoke.

Clyde laughed and said, "Morning, Woodie," a nickname Woodrow hated. "What kinda work you got today for the best motor-grader operator in Louisiana?"

Woodrow couldn't help but laugh. He'd heard about the tussle at Luke Faucheaux's joint the night before.

"If you mean work for the Louisiana wrestling champ, we ain't got shit. But if you're talking about Norma Fitzhugh's husband, Clyde, well, I just might have something," Woodrow said smiling.

A big smirk on Woodrow's face almost undid Clyde. He was reminded of the time before he won Norma's heart that Woodrow had really been sweet on her.

A one-sided affection but to this day the thought still got Clyde's dander up. But he held back thinking to himself, *You dumb bastard, I got the woman and all you got is the lard ass your sitting on.*

He needed the job, so he laughed off the remark and said, "What'cha got, Woodrow?"

"You know the back road to Jackson Landing, running off Hwy 19? Well, we got that old grader sitting over in Ralph Pinkney's field waiting for you to crank her up and grade that poor-excuse-for-a-parish road. Want that?" Woodrow asked.

Clyde said, "Give me the keys, and I'm on my way."

Woodrow replied, "Hell, the damn keys are in it. Ain't no one dumb enough to steal that piece of junk."

Clyde winced; he loved the old beater and was the only one in the parish who could skin 1-inch of clay on a back road with one pass of the old blade.

"I'll be on my way; give my regards to Gertrude," said Clyde as he made his way out the door.

Gertrude was Woodrow's simpleton wife with looks worthy of a mule that had just been hit with a 2x4, an unfortunate fact that Woodrow knew, and Clyde liked to provoke.

He quickly walked out to the Skylark and started her up. He gunned the big V-8 and let it rip out of the gravel parking lot heading for Jackson Landing. It didn't take long at 75 mph, 50 on the dirt road. Clyde found the old Caterpillar grader parked off the side of road in a barren cotton field.

He parked the Bird, his name for his little Skylark, and walked over to the old grader. He checked the oil, tires and fuel gauge and decided she was ready to work. He cranked the engine over a few times to loosen her up, pumped the accelerator twice, turned the key and the big diesel fired up.

He smiled and thought, *The old gal's still got it.* After checking to make sure the grading blade was raised, he put it in gear and drove the big machine onto the dirt road.

Getting a straight path aligned, he lowered the blade and eye-balled it to make sure his cut was not too deep. Slowly, the big wheels of the grader began to move as the angled scraper cut the ruts in the dirt road to an even plane.

Looking behind him, Clyde could see the new smooth surface each cut made, but he knew the road would be rutted out again in two months from rain and traffic.

He turned back to the front as he crested a small rise in the road and came upon a wagon being drawn by two mules. Clyde carefully moved to the oncoming side of the road barely missing the wagon. He waved at the old black man driving the wagon, Moses Jones.

Clyde had grown up with Moses. Both men were showing signs of age but hard work and hard living had been their life. And both men knew it.

Clyde hollered, "Moses, how you doin'? You workin' them mules hard or are you hardly workin'?"

Moses yelled back laughing, "Why, Mr. Clyde, when'd you ever seen a twenty-year-old mule that ain't working as hard at that old grader you be driving?"

Clyde laughed hard and said, "Moses, you right as rain. Come by and see us soon. I got a hankerin' to laugh about the long-gone days. So make it soon and take care. You call on that new talkie thing Ms. Norma got if you get some trouble to stirrin'."

"Yassuh, Mr. Clyde, you knows I got your number," replied Moses, both men laughing but knowing full well Clyde was talking about the 'Klan mess' as he called it.

Clyde goosed the old grader on down the road.

Time drifted lazily by as the grader slowly made the old road look almost new. With a mile to go before, he would hit pavement on the outskirts of Jackson Landing, he saw a red pickup truck in the ditch off the side of the road.

The truck was laying sideways, and the driver's side had hit and knocked over several large pine trees. Clyde stopped and quickly jumped out of the tractor cab and ran over to the wrecked truck.

It didn't look good. The driver was obviously dead. His head smashed completely through the windshield. Clyde noticed that the man's face was almost unrecognizable. Blood covered the upper body, which had been severely crushed by the steering wheel. Clyde didn't know the driver.

He heard some moaning. Looking across the driver's body, he saw a young girl pushed under the passenger side of the truck's dashboard. Quickly, he ran to the other side of the truck and tried to pull the door open. The truck was stuck deep in the lower side of the ditch but the passenger side window was open.

"Can you hear me?" Clyde asked the girl, hoping for a response.

She cried out saying, "Lord, just help my baby."

Panicked, Clyde pulled on the passenger door with all his strength. Opening the door enough to put his hand through, he touched the girl's arm. She yelled in pain. Her arm was broken. Looking closer, he could see part of her bone sticking through her skin.

"Can you sit up?" He asked.

"I's stuck and my baby is beside me. Help me, oh God, please help me," she pleaded.

"You lay still. I'll be right back," Clyde promised.

He climbed up the side of the ditch and saw Moses coming down the road. He waved, cupped his hands and hollered, "Moses, come quick. I need your help. Hurry!"

Moses got the mules into a trot, and the old wagon followed behind. He quickly reached the wrecked truck and pulled the mules to a stop. Moses looked at the truck and said, "Lord have mercy, Mr. Clyde; what don happen here?"

"There's a girl alive and stuck in the truck. Driver's dead. You got any rope we can tie on the truck and pull it out to get to the girl and her baby?" Clyde asked.

"Lord, Mr. Clyde! There be a baby in that ol truck too?" Moses replied as he stared at the demolished truck.

"Yes, now you got a rope?" Clyde repeated, not taking his eyes off the wrecked truck.

"Yassuh, I gots one, but I dasn't know how youse gonna get that ol truck out. My mules can do it, but I gots to get them outa harness," Moses replied.

Clyde said, "No time for that. I'll tie the rope to the back of the grader and see if I can move the truck without hurting the girl and baby."

Moses climbed into his wagon and found the rope, which he handed down to Clyde who quickly walked down to the truck and tied the rope around the bumper. Stretching the rope as close to the grader as he could, he jumped in the grader, cranked her up and backed it to the rope.

Moses picked up the rope and tied a loop to hold fast and attached it to the grader. Then Clyde said to Moses, "You go down and watch the passenger door. I'm gonna pull on the truck and the door should get caught on the side of the ditch and pull open. When it's open enough to get her out, wave your arms and I'll come help you."

"Yassuh, ol Moses be watchin'."

Clyde stepped up to the driver's seat of the old grader and put it in gear, slowly moving forward. The rope tightened and stretched as the truck slowly moved backward, angling up the side of the ditch. The passenger door caught in the mud and began to open as the truck was dragged.

Moses began waving his arms and yelled, "That's got it, the door be open good, I can see the young girl and the baby." After Clyde stopped the grader, he jumped from the cab and ran to Moses who anxiously said, "I think we can get them out the truck if we hurry, but we best watch that old rope."

Leaning in, Clyde calmed the girl and asked for her name. She moaned, "I be Nell."

"We're going to get you and your baby out and take y'all to the doctor, so be brave; this may hurt," Clyde said calmly.

She moaned, "Yassuh, jes help my baby."

Clyde did not see the baby and did not know if it survived the crash. He turned to Moses and said, "Let's get her out and take her up to your wagon. Can you take her into town?"

Moses replied, "Why I s'pect so. I gots some bags of feed in my wagon, but I thinks she be alright a layin' on them till I gets to town."

Slowly, they pulled the girl toward the door, and Moses held her legs while Clyde picked up her body, trying to avoid the broken arm. She yelled in pain as they got her to the side of the road. Then she pleaded, "Please get my baby."

Clyde jumped down the side of the ditch, hurried to the side of the truck and looked for Nell's baby. The little baby boy was laying on his back asleep. Clyde thought he was dead, but the little boy opened his eyes and smiled.

Relieved, Clyde reached down, picked him up and carried him up the steep bank of the ditch. He told Nell, "I got him for ya. He's fine and can ride with you into town," he assured her.

The two men placed the girl in the back of the wagon and tried to make her as comfortable as possible. Then they put the baby, next to her. Clyde turned to Moses and said, "I'm goin' to get the grader going fast as I can to get you a smooth ride into town. If I get too far ahead, I'll get someone from the doctor's office to ride out and meet you."

Moses responded, "I'm gonna be following hard. I know this gal is hurt really bad. But we'll make it. We gots to make it."

Clyde said nothing as he turned and cut the rope with his knife. He then climbed into the cab, lowered the grader blade and headed for Jackson Landing.

The old grader was going as fast as he could push it with the blade down. As he smoothed the road, Moses had the mules pulling at a slow trot. Gradually, the grader pulled ahead, but Moses kept the mules at a trot with the old wagon, shaking and creaking as if it would come apart at any moment.

Clyde reached the edge of town and pulled into the Esso station owned by Junior Thompson. He jumped down from the grader just as Junior was walking toward him hollering, "Clyde, get that damn thing outta here. You're gonna block my customers."

"Junior, I gotta use your phone, there's been a bad wreck. I got Moses Jones bringing in a girl and her baby. The girl's in bad shape but the baby seems ok. I need to get a hold of that new doctor. What the hell is his name?"

Junior said, "Montgomery. Only been here for a few weeks since Doc Preston up and retired. Kinda whacky-doodle guy if you ask me. Come here from some little piss-ant town in the Mississippi Delta. Come on in and use the phone. These folks I might know?"

"I doubt it," said Clyde. "Where's the damn phone?"

Junior pointed. Clyde picked up and dialed the operator who connected him to Doctor Montgomery's office.

"This is Clyde Fitzhugh. I'm down at Junior Thompson's Esso station, and we need an ambulance. Had a car wreck and got a woman and baby that needs help."

The voice on the other end replied, "Well, I'll get the doctor soon as I can, and I'll get the ambulance there as soon as possible. How bad are the people hurt?"

"One's got a bad broken arm and elsewise pretty beat up. The baby seems in pretty good shape. Just get the ambulance down here," Clyde demanded.

"Alright, now, again who are you and where are you?" the receptionist questioned.

"I'm Clyde Fitzhugh, I'm at Junior Davis's Esso station across from the parish courthouse. Get to moving damnit."

"Well, you don't gotta curse like that," the receptionist said rolling her eyes.

"If that goddamn ambulance ain't here in 5 minutes, you'll be seeing me in 10," yelled Clyde.

With that, he said, "Damned peckerwoods," slammed the phone down looked at Junior and hollered, "here comes Moses. Junior, get some water, I'm sure that girl and the baby are parched to the bone."

Junior reached under the counter where his favorite bourbon was hidden and got some big paper cups. He filled them to the brim with water and handed them to Clyde. Moses slowed his mules that were lathered good from the trot to the gas station.

Nell was passed out in the back of the wagon with the baby asleep, lying on her unbroken arm. Clyde climbed into the wagon. He lifted Nell's head carefully and put the cup of water to her mouth. She moaned and cried in pain.

"Drink slowly," Clyde said gently.

She drank until the cup was empty before asking, "My baby?"

"He's right next to you," Clyde said as he lifted the child's head. "I'm going to give him some water. He's gonna be fine. The doc is on his way."

Finally, they heard the ambulance siren and saw an old white Cadillac hearse now used as an ambulance pull into the gas station. Junior was busy moving cars around, and then saw Clyde lift Nell's head and went running over to the wagon.

He leaned up and said, "Clyde you probably don't know 'bout this new doc; he say he won't work on colored folk."

Clyde looked down and said, "Junior, you go call Sheriff Cummings and tell him I'm here, and I need him here fast. You got that?"

"Sure do, Mr. Clyde. I know exactly what you want," Junior said as he quickly made his way to the phone.

As he ran to call the sheriff, he passed the ambulance driver who'd just pulled in to the gas station. Junior quickly told him, "You best be on good behavior; that man in that wagon helpin' those folk is Clyde Fitzhugh."

The driver was the new doctor's brother-in-law. He looked at Clyde helping Nell. He turned to Junior, and said, "I don't give a shit who he is. The doc says he don't work on colored folk."

Junior replied, "Tell that to the sheriff; he'll be here any minute. I ain't saying nothing else. If you want to cross a Fitzhugh, well you done picked the wrong one."

Clyde climbed down from the wagon and walked toward the ambulance. He approached the driver and said, "Come on over here and give me a hand. I need help with this girl."

The driver looked at him and said, "Doc Montgomery don't fool with no colored folk. You gonna have to take her somewhere else."

Clyde walked close and looked the driver eyeball to eyeball and said, "You didn't hear what I said, did you?"

Stunned by the demand, the driver cautiously said, "Yeah, I heard you; what do you want to do about it?"

Just before the whooping was about to start, Sheriff Cummings drove up knowing full well what was about to take place. He quickly got out of the car and walked briskly over to the two men.

"Clyde, you called what's going on?" The sheriff asked.

Clyde said, "Ben, there's a bad truck wreck back down the dirt road toward Greenwood. Young gal and her baby made it. The driver's dead. Truck's about mile and-a-half outside of Jackson Landing. Moses Jones and I got the gal and her baby cut and got them this far."

"Called the new doctor and ambulance. Then, this here no-count, son-of-bitch shows up and tells me the new doc won't work on colored folk."

The driver winced at the remark and said, "Now just a damn minute."

But the sheriff looked straight at him and cut him off before he could finish, "Did I ask you something?"

The man stammered and said nothing as the sheriff said, "So keep your mouth shut; now here's what's gonna happen. You're gonna do whatever Mr. Fitzhugh asks you to do. You got that, boy?"

The driver stared at Clyde and said, "I understand but the doc ain't gonna like it one bit."

"I'll handle the doctor," assured the sheriff. "Now get that woman and her baby in the ambulance and get them to the clinic."

Clyde, Moses and the driver got in the wagon. They carefully lifted Nell and carried her to the ambulance.

Clyde picked up the baby and handed him down to Junior who carried him to the ambulance and got in the passenger's side.

Junior said, "I'll carry the baby. Sheriff, we gonna follow you? I don't want no trouble with that new doc, but I sure don't want a miss an ass whoopin' if Clyde's doin' the whoopin'."

"Gotcha covered; now let's get going," said the sheriff.

Then turning to the ambulance driver, he said, "Boy, you follow me, and you best be fast, so turn on your damn siren. And, Junior, you make damn sure this redneck gets that siren going and movin' fast."

Sheriff Cummings thought to himself, *Asshole, Mississippi rednecks; probably in the damn Klan.*

Clyde walked over to Moses and said, "Thanks, Moses. I wouldn't done any good on my own."

Moses looked at Clyde and said, "Mr. Clyde, I'm always ready to help a Fitzhugh."

"And you know your family has always been special to us. Lord, how many years do we go back?" Clyde said.

"Lordy, Mr. Clyde, too long for ol Moses to member," Moses said smiling to himself.

"Well, I best call the sheriff's office and tell Ms. Ruth to be waiting for the sheriff to call. Then I'm heading down to the wrecked truck," said Clyde.

After the call to his sister, Ruth, Clyde checked the old grader, got a Grapette from Junior's cooler and sat down for a rest.

The sheriff pulled his new Plymouth car with 'Sheriff' written on three sides into the clinic's dirt parking lot. Sheriff Cummings was damn proud of the new Plymouth.

Modified to police standards, it would do 120 mph with plenty of engine left. Damn fast in 1962 for a Plymouth Savoy.

If the California Patrol boys liked these hot toys, then the sheriff had to have one. And he got it.

Sheriff Cummings piled out of the car like the hardass he really was. Sparks in his eyes made it well known to those who knew him, he was ready for any smartass looking for his kind of justice.

The ambulance pulled in, as the driver got out and walked to the clinic office. Doctor Montgomery came rushing out the door with his nurse following close behind.

Sheriff Cummings said, "Doc, we got a woman in your ambulance needs help real bad and real quick. Broken arm and God knows what else. Want to take a look afore we bring her in?"

Junior got out of the sheriffs car saying, "Lordy, don't forget about the baby."

Doctor Montgomery looked at the baby then into the side windows of the old ambulance. He turned to the sheriff and said, "We don't treat niggers here, Sheriff."

Sheriff Cummings looked at him hard and said, "Now, I ain't a askin'. I'm a tellin'."

The doc looked shocked and replied, "Where I come from, there's a distinct difference tween niggers and whites."

"Well," said Sheriff Cummings, "let me just guess where your dumb ass comes from."

With that, he spit out a large spray of tobacco juice at the foot of the doctor. The sheriff chewed on the job, a habit his wife wouldn't allow at home. "You look like one of those Delta rednecks that don't know shit from shinola. Am I right?"

The doctor stammered and turned scarlet with humiliation. Sheriff Cummings looked hard at the doctor and said, "Now here's what's gonna happen. Your boy drivin' that piece-of-shit ambulance is goin' to help your nurse get that young gal and her baby into your clinic, and fix her up real good and real polite like."

"It's that simple. You listening, Doc? Cause your eyes look like you're thinking bullshit. Am I right?"

The doc said, "Well, this is my clinic, and I'll run it like I run all my clinics."

Sheriff Cummings responded, "You mean like those dumps you call clinics in the Mississippi Delta?"

"What do you know about my clinics?" The doc nervously said.

"Hell, who doesn't know 'bout those no-good, run-down shacks you call clinics. Why, I know enough to shut you down here and in Mississippi if you don't abide by my rules. And let me explain somethin' else to you, Clyde Fitzhugh brought these folk in from a truck wreck."

"He told me he's got a special interest in their well-being. You do know the Fitzhughs, right?" The sheriff asked in a raised voice.

"No never heard of 'em and don't really give a damn who or what they want," the doctor replied, trying to stand his ground.

The sheriff replied with a sharp edge to his voice, "You ever hear of a barn burner?"

Doc Montgomery simply said, "No."

"Well, Mr. Clyde's papa, old man Fitzhugh, used to have a way of getting even with folks that crossed him. Sometime late at night or early morning, if you crossed the old man, you might wake up in the middle of the night to a blaze a burnin' your barn, your cotton field or your tractor."

"Or your new car won't start cuz there's sand in the gas tank. And you'll never know who done it. But no one in this parish ever crossed that old man. And everything I just told you may or may not be true. You hear me, you goddamn Mississippi redneck son-of-a bitch?" The sheriff yelled, mad as hell.

"You want Clyde Fitzhugh and his older brother, Son, on your ass? If you do then you best pack your bags and get the hell out of this Parish and maybe the state, cuz if I leave and you ain't helpin' that young woman, I gotta call Clyde and let him know the trouble you've caused, and let you do the splainin' to him and his brother, Son Fitzhugh."

The doctor looked at the nurse and the driver and said, "Get the young lady and the baby into the clinic." He looked at the sheriff and said, "You tell Mr. Fitzhugh I'll do my best to make sure she and her baby are well cared for."

Sheriff Cummings smiled while digging into a pack of Red Man tobacco and simply said, "Thanks, Doc. I know you'll do your best work on this here gal and her baby. I gotta go; I'm sure Mr. Fitzhugh has been calling the office's looking for me. I'll tell him the good news."

With that, Sheriff Cummings sprayed another wad of tobacco juice, just missing the doctor's feet. "Pretty good chaw. I ain't spit that fast and that far since my wife curn near caught me chewing in my garage. Well, get her fixed up real good and the Fitzhughs may leave you be. I'll be seein' you soon, Doc."

The sheriff used the radio to his patrol station and was patched in to the phone at Junior's Esso station. Clyde was cranking up the old grader when Junior's helper came running out and yelled, "Sheriff's on the phone."

Sheriff Cummings told Clyde about scaring the hell out of the doctor and his so-called employees with the old Fitzhugh story. Clyde laughed so hard he liked to drop the phone, "Well, Ben, I'm heading back to the wreck. You got that deputy of yours on his way?"

"Should be there already. You best crank the grader and get going. Thanks, Clyde, you done good by them folks."

Clyde cranked up the grader and headed west. About a mile out from Jackson Landing, Clyde saw the deputy and a state trooper's car. He pulled off the side of the road into the field, climbed down from the grader and walked to the two cops standing on the side of the road looking at the wrecked truck. What looked like a body covered with a white cloth was lying next to the truck.

The state trooper looked at Clyde and said, "Well, hell if it ain't Mr. Fitzhugh."

Clyde looked at him and said, "That's Clyde to you, Melvin. How the hell have you been? Taking care of that pretty wife of yours or do you need some help?"

The trooper laughed and said, "Norma would be on you like a Catahoula hog dog on the hunt."

They both laughed. Clyde said, "You got that right, Melvin. So, what's it look like to you, Deputy?"

The deputy jokingly replied, "Name's Jim as if you didn't know. Sarcastic redneck."

Clyde laughed hard and started coughing, "Ha, Jim, you finally got something right today. But no shit what the hell you boys think happened?"

"Well," Melvin said. "Looks like the old negra that was driving, he was pretty damn drunk, passed out and ran into that clump of pines. Knocked five of 'em clean over. Must been doing about 50. Sound about right, Jim?"

"Yep," Melvin's partner Jim said. "I knew this one. Name was Watson. Worked for Ms. Ruth and Ms. Robbye."

"Well, I'll be damned," Clyde said. "You know they're both my close kin."

"Yep," Jim said. "We'll have to pay them a visit soon as the body is picked up by the state boys. The state's the only ones got a morgue. Maybe while we wait, you could drive back to Jackson Landing and let them know we'd like to have a friendly talk and see if they can help figure out what's what. What about the young girl and baby?"

"Moses Jones helped me get them to the doc in town. They seemed busted up pretty good but basically they should be ok," said Clyde.

"So, how'd you get that new doctor to work on colored folk?" The deputy asked.

"Hell," Clyde said. "I just told him to do his job or get out of town."

"Tough talk from a Fitzhugh," the trooper chimed in.

"Got his attention! He got to work like a hound on the scent. He was working like the fear of God was about to lay him out. And that God's name would be Clyde Fitzhugh," laughed Clyde.

They all laughed, and Jim choked out, "Clyde, you're one tough Irishman."

"The blessing of Jesus, Joseph and Mary be upon you all," Clyde joked as he climbed into the Yellow Bird.

He started the engine and hit the gas as he popped the clutch and sped down the road toward Jackson Landing. Ruth and Robbye had best be around he thought as he hit 60 on the dirt road. He arrived at the parish courthouse where both women worked. He parked and walked into the tax assessor's office.

Ruth Stanley, Clyde's sister, was sitting at her desk. She looked up and said, "Well, if it ain't baby brother, also known as trouble. What brings you to town without Norma in tow?"

Norma and Ruth were far from being on good terms. Ruth's divorced husband was a Stanley and Clyde's drinking buddy whenever they thought they were still young, raucous and just plain wild-ass country boys. Norma did not like the Stanley clan then or now.

"Go get Sister," said Clyde. "Now!" Sister was the family name for Robbye.

Ruth saw he was serious and said, "What's going on?"

"Just go get her and meet me upstairs in the courtroom where we can talk in private."

Ruth walked into the Clerk of Courts office and told Robbye, "Follow me."

"Clyde's upstairs and looks mighty damn serious."

Robbye got up from her desk and followed Ruth out into the atrium of the parish hall and up the stairs to the empty courtroom. The two women pushed the heavy wooden doors open and found Clyde sitting on the prosecutor's table. Ruth said, "Ok, Baby brother, what's the big story today?"

"That durn fool you had working on your place wrecked his damn truck about half a mile from your house and killed his damn self."

"Oh my God," gasped Robbye. "Was anyone else hurt?"

"Yeah," said Clyde. "That young colored gal he kept locked up in that shack down by your place was pretty banged up, but her baby seemed to be fine. Moses Jones helped me get them out of that junked-up truck and into town to the new doctor's office."

"Thank God Nell wasn't hurt," said Robbye with a sigh of relief.

"Well, she has a pretty bad broken arm and was bleeding poorly from her female parts, so I don't know how all of that will turn out. I had a few problems with the new sawbones, but he came around and decided he could work on colored folk," Clyde said.

Then he glared at them both and said, "So now here's the problem for you two, Big Sister and Sister. That gal and baby are gonna need help and since your no-count negra damn near killed them both. I suspect ya'll gonna need to help her out with some money and a place to stay."

"Now wait just a damn minute," Ruth sharply said, "yes, the son-of-a-bitch worked for us, and yes, we tried to help out the young gal he called his wife, but we didn't volunteer to take care of her forever."

Clyde looked down at Ruth and said, "It's your problem, and you best fix it cause in about 2 hours, it's going to be the talk of the town. Sheriff Cummings has his deputies on the hunt, and they're gonna want to know how come these folks were heading for Greenwood in the middle of the night and Christ knows that some of the redneck Klan bunch will be talking trash."

Ruth smirked at Robbye saying, "I told ya no good deed goes unpunished."

Robbye scowled at Ruth and said, "Big Papa was right; you always were a smartass woman."

Clyde looked at them puffing at each other and started to laugh, "Ooh-whee, are we gonna see a cat fight in the judge's chambers? Now calm down and let's figure out how to help this gal and her baby. Let's make it right for the baby at least."

"I have no respect for any man that treats a woman the way you both said he treated that young gal. So, calm down. Ruth, you need to go check on her and the baby at the clinic. Robbye and I will meet you later at the Big House and discuss this over a drink and something to eat."

"Someone call Norma and have her pick up some fried chicken from that new chicken joint in Angola. We'll talk this thing through and come up with something that'll work for all. Agreed?"

Both women nodded their heads yes. Ruth said, "I'll be there at 6pm sharp. And, Clyde, don't you get to drinking before I get there."

"I won't lessen your no-count Stanley relatives show up. If they do, we'll all be off to New Orleans and leave y'all to figure this mess out," Clyde said as he gave another raucous laugh.

Ruth looked angrily at him but didn't say a word. Robbye said, "I'll call Norma and let her know about the food, and we'll be at the house around 6:00. Is that good for all?"

All nodded agreement. Clyde and Robbye walked to Clyde's car. They both got in and started the back-road drive toward Greenwood. Robbye said just before they slowed down the accident scene. "I don't think I can look at Watson's dead body."

Clyde told her to stay in the car that he'd take care of any details. The deputy had called a wrecker, no doubt from Junior's garage. Watson's old truck was on the back of the flatbed truck already pulling away.

Clyde slowed to a stop next to the deputy and hollered out the window, "So the state boys left you in charge?"

"Yep," replied the deputy, "said it was a parish resident on a parish road and was a parish problem. So, I'm here to clean up the mess. Somehow I always end up with the crap jobs."

Clyde said, "Well, Jim, shit do flow downhill. They take the body?"

The deputy replied, "Yep it was getting kinda ripe in this heat. Good thing Ms. Robbye didn't have to see the mess that damn fool made."

Clyde said, "Keep up the good work, Jim. You might be sheriff one day." He waved and hit the gas pedal and they went flying down the road. "Sister, I've got to stop at the Highway Barn and give old Woodie the lowdown and punch the time clock," said Clyde.

Robbye laughed, "I'm sure he'll be glad to know you were doing something productive for a change."

Clyde laughed at Robbye's remark. After a few miles of quiet time, Clyde turned into the Highway yard and deliberately slammed on the brakes causing a cloud of dust to rise up and over the small office building. Woodrow stood at the window scowling as Clyde got out, slammed the car door and ran to the office.

"Woodrow, it's been the damndest day I've had in years," Clyde hollered.

Woodrow was a bit put out but concerned as he stood by the window. Taking his cigar from his mouth he said, "How so? You didn't whoop somebody or worse flip the damn grader?"

"Naw, nothing that fun. Why this mornin' as I was gradin' that damn washboard road to Jackson Landing when I came on a bad truck wreck. Stopped, went down to the wreck and there was this no-count fool hangin' out the front windshield deader than a Kansas preacher's pecker. Next to him was this young gal and baby."

"Girl was hurt but the baby was fine. Had to get help and get them to the new idiot they call a doctor. Then I had to meet the sheriff and get the mess cleaned up. A hell of a day," Clyde explained.

Woodrow looked at him suspiciously and said, "Clyde, you're not bullshitting me, are you?"

"As God's my witness, all is true; just ask Ben. Now I best punch the clock and get to the house. Got meet with kin folk who that sumbitch worked for and get the lowdown before all hell breaks loose," said Clyde heading to the time clock.

"Well, get going," said Woodie. "And if you need some help with the sheriff, let me know. He is my brother-in-law."

Clyde, being uncharacteristically polite to Woodrow, said, "Thanks, Boss. I'll remember the offer."

Clyde and Robbye sped out of the yard onto the highway as Clyde goosed the Bird up to 80. Made it home in about 12 minutes. *Thank goodness,* he thought, *Norma ain't home yet.* "Robbye, you wait in the kitchen. I'll be there in just a minute."

He parked and walked around the side of the house heading for the dog pen. He pulled out his bottle of Old Granddad and took a drink long enough to knock most men flat. When it was re-corked and hid, he turned, walked back to the porch and pulled up a bucket of water.

He washed his face and hands, gargled a glass full of water, dried off and walked into the kitchen just in time to hear the screen door slam. "Clyde," Norma yelled, "you here?"

"Back in the kitchen, darlin', with Sister. Ruth will be here by 6," Clyde yelled back.

"Now someone tell me what in the hell is going on," demanded Norma. Clyde explained his day and his concerns about the wreck. "Well," Norma said, "I got food, and I know you have that damn bottle out by the dog pen so go get it. Sister, can you help me set some kinda decent table?"

"Yes," she said. "Just show me the way," said Robbye.

Clyde was shaken as he walked out to the 'hidey hole' as he called it. How the hell did Norma know about the bottle? "That woman knows me better than I know myself."

He picked up the log, grabbed the bottle and walked back to the house and into the kitchen. It was coming on to 6pm when Ruth walked into the kitchen and said, "Well, what are we all here for?"

Clyde said, "Well hell-o to you too. What did you find at that no-count clinic?"

"Doc said her arm was busted good and that she was pregnant but lost the baby in the wreck," responded Ruth.

"We gotta figure out how Ben Cummings is gonna sort this mess of a wreck out. That gal and the dead fool that went through the windshield were working for you and Sister. Ain't that right?" Clyde said stroking his chin thinking about a possible inquiry by the sheriff or state troopers.

"Yes, the negra's name was Watson. Don't know him by any other name 'cept Watson. He was working for us doing odd jobs around the farm. Had that young woman kept in a shack on the property."

"Treated her like she was some sort of slave. Imagine that, a colored man with a slave," said Ruth as she chuckled to herself.

Clyde looked at her sternly and said, "Ain't no laughing matter, Ruth. A man's dead and the sheriff's gonna want to know where he came from and what they were doing driving down the back road and that sum bitch drunk with the gal and a baby in the truck."

"And then the question will be who's gonna pay the cost of hauling the truck, burying the dead man and care for the young gal. I s'pect they's gonna be looking at you and Robbye to help out since he was your man."

Ruth looked harshly at Clyde, "Well, we weren't his keeper. He took off in the middle of the night. I had a run in with him two days ago when he was threatening our nephews Tom and Will with a razor."

Clyde said, "So you did run him off."

"Well," Ruth said, "I didn't tell him to get off the property. I told him to get right with his work and his family. Guess he didn't like my suggestion, so he took off. Can't put no blame on us."

"Norma, pass me some of that new-fangled chicken. I'm starving. What they call that chicken?"

"Kentucky Fried; supposed to have some secret recipe," replied Norma.

"Not bad for store bought," Ruth said as she took a bite.

"Alright," Clyde said, "enough chicken talk. We've got to get our story straight no matter who's asking the questions. But one more thing, Ruth, you said that the dead man pulled a razor on Tommy and Will?"

Ruth replied, "You're damn right he did. Nell, his wife, was trying to run off and Tommy and Will stopped him from chasin' her."

Clyde slowly said, "If need be, that could work in our favor. But for now, let's keep it amongst ourselves. We all talk as one. Agreed?"

They all agreed. "And we also need to do something about that young gal and her baby," Clyde added.

"Why do you have such an interest in helping out some young colored gal?" Norma said.

When speaking of people of color, the word 'colored' was most polite. 'Negra' derogatory, but 'nigger' was down-right insulting. Regardless, Clyde knew what was coming next.

Norma smugly said, "We always knew you had a hankerin' for the dark side. Ain't that right, darlin'?"

Clyde pushed his chair back, stood up and stared at Norma, who stared right back at him. A big mistake on her part. Clyde turned crimson red, his dark eyes flashing with sparks as he said, "You say another word, Norma, Fitzhugh, and you'll regret that kinda talk for the rest of your life."

Norma looked at him headstrong as hell, staring back at him but she didn't say a word. Ruth and Robbye sat quietly, heads down. They all knew the story of Clyde being sweet on a black girl when he was much younger and well before he met Norma. The young girl had a child. The girl died when the man her mother lived with killed her during a family argument.

The young girl had a baby and the small-town rumor mill went wild about Clyde and the girl, until Big Papa Fitzhugh put a rough end to the gossip.

Norma's comment was no off-handed jibe; it was a serious punch to the gut, and Clyde couldn't let it pass. They all remained quiet as Clyde reached for the Old Grandad, pulled the cork and drank deep.

He sat down, staring with a furious intensity at Norma, and said, "Now I've had enough of this horseshit. I found these folks on the road. They came from Robbye and Ruth's. A baby was in the truck. I found out from the sheriff that the young girl was also pregnant and lost her baby in the wreck."

"That's what I know. Now if you bunch of women want to explain to Ben Cummings how all this mess happened to these two black folk that worked for you, Ruth and Robbye, then I don't give a good goddamn what happens next. I'll be damned if I have to listen to insults from my wife who can bark loud but can't give me children."

Norma looked at him and whispered, "I'm sorry. I shouldn't have been so rude. I'm truly sorry. Please, can you forgive me?"

They all looked at Clyde. He sat straight up in his chair wringing his big, rough hands while not taking his eyes off of Norma. "Never again," he said.

"You mention my past life again in front of my blood kin and that will be the end of you and me. I mean it. I work hard, I give you a home, I love you and yet you spit at me like a cornered rattlesnake. It stops now. Swear in front of Ruth and Robbye, NEVER AGAIN!"

Norma anxiously looked at Ruth and Robbye for support then at Clyde and with tears swelling up in her eyes said, "I swear never again."

Clyde reached out and touched her, as tears eased down her face. He gently smiled. He and Norma had always been deeply in love no matter the ferocity in the way they would sometimes speak to each other.

Changing his tone, Clyde quickly spoke to all saying, "So we've settled on the no-count bastard that abused her. Now what do we do help the young girl? She's hurt bad and is going to need some place to stay."

Robbye was first to talk. She told the story of Nell and Mam, and how she and Ruth decided to try and help Nell get a better place to raise her child. Watson had come with the deal.

Ruth spoke up and suggested, "What about Aunt Sue? She lives down the road across from Son and Eva's. She's been with our family for years. And she helps with colored children in need of a decent upbringing."

Ruth, chewing the last bite of her chicken, continued, "I think it's worth considering. Clyde, would you pour me a whiskey and ginger ale, please?"

Clyde passed the drink to Ruth, who took a big drink, washed it around in her mouth, then swallowed. She said, "I think my idea might just solve a lot of problems. The girl and her baby boy would have a safe home, and if we all put some money in Aunt Sue's pocket to help, why I think she'd be mighty happy. Clyde, what do you think?"

Clyde looked at Norma and said, "What about it, Norma. Is that ok with you?"

They all stared at Norma. Her neck was flush red and her voice cracked as she said, "I think that would be the right thing to do."

"That's settled," said Clyde. "Norma, can you get with Eva and talk to Aunt Sue. I think we should all chip in and help Aunt Sue with her expenses."

They all agreed. Then the telephone rang three times. Clyde and Norma looked at each other and Clyde said, "I'll get it."

He walked quickly to the old telephone. Eva was working the switchboard.

She stammered, "Clyde, are you there?"

"Yes, Eva, what can I do for you?" He casually replied.

"I got the sheriff on the line, and he wants to have a word with you about some sort of accident," explained Eva.

"Yeah, I know all about it. Put him through," responded Clyde.

"Clyde, you there? This is Ben," said the sheriff.

"Yeah, Ben. Eva told me. What do you need?" Clyde asked.

"Well," Ben said. "The state troopers wanted a full report on the accident that happened today, and I thought you might shed a little light on things to help get them off my back."

Clyde said. "I thought your deputy told me the troopers said it was a parish issue. How come they're so curious now?"

"Hell if I know. Something about a call they received from that new doctor," Ben replied.

"Well, what the hell did he tell them?"

"I don't know for sure. Something about that girl from the wreck being kept like a slave. Locked up all day and not getting any help or money from Ms. Robbye or Ruth," Ben said reluctantly.

Raising his voice, Clyde said, "That's a damn lie and you know it, Ben. I reckon I need to have a serious talk with the new doc. But first, Ben, let me give you a quick rundown on how things really were."

"That young girl was living out at Mam's place past the crossroad cut off. She lived in that old shack with the big cotton field around it. You know the place?"

"Sure," Ben said. "That's the place where John DeLee drops off all them colored kids he finds throughout the parish. Supposed to be outcast or on their own," he said with a smirk.

"That's the place," Clyde said. "So Robbye was personally helping that gal out and in the whole mix this half-drunk negra man named Watson showed up wanting to take the girl for himself. Mam had said she just couldn't handle any more children."

"Robbye and Ruth found out and told Mam that they had a job for the man and a place where they could stay. The man seemed to be working pretty good for a while, then he started hitting the bottle and started to hittin' on the young gal too. And she being pregnant and all at the time."

Ben said, "That no good bastard was beating on a pregnant girl?"

"Yep," Clyde replied. "Then he pulled a razor on my nephews, Tommy and Will. So Ruth confronts him about locking the gal up during the day when he was out hustling some poor soul or drinking, and then back to roughing up the girl and threatening my nephews."

"Ruth gave him a choice with her .38. Stop locking up the gal up, threatening people and get his ass to work. Well, apparently, he didn't take that to well, so he took off in the middle of the night with the young girl and the baby. Driving drunk, he ran the old truck into a tree."

"Went through the windshield and killed his black-ass self. Thank God, the girl and baby were ok. Enough information?"

"Yeah," Ben said, "except one more thing. The pregnant girl. Was the baby Watson's or maybe someone else's?"

Clyde stood stone still and slowly said, "Just what do you mean by that question, Ben?"

"Why nothing, Clyde. Just something the doctor asked."

"I see," Clyde said. "Guess I need to pay that doc a visit sooner rather than later."

"Now, Clyde, don't go doing anything foolish. I think the girl can answer this question pretty easy, and it will all pass. What's your plan?" Ben asked.

"Funny you should ask. We're all sitting here, and I think we've come up with something to help her out. I'll stop by tomorrow on my way to see the doc and tell you all about it. What's a good time?" Clyde said.

"Say first thing in the morning, 'bout 7:30?" Ben answered.

"We'll be there. And, Ben, if you want to go with me to the doc's, you're more than welcome. See ya at 7:30 sharp."

With that, Clyde hung up the phone.

While Clyde was on the phone, Norma was busy telling Robbye and Ruth how sorry she was for the outburst of anger they'd heard. "Y'all don't know 'bout any of this and you best never repeat it," whispered Norma.

Both women looked anxiously at Norma. Ruth finally said, "Is this about not having children?"

Norma replied, "As a matter of fact, Ruth, it is. It's about Clyde and me. Clyde always thought I was not able to have children. But I was at the lady doctor in Baton Rouge several years ago, and she told me I could. Said I was fertile as any other healthy gal."

"So, I thought hell, if it ain't me, it's got to be Clyde. But I wasn't 'bout to tell him. I knew all 'bout the story of him and that young black girl from years ago. But I figured, bygones be bygone."

"But I know it grates the hell out him to think about it, so now and then, I throw it out to light a fire. But I know and he knows that the real truth is I'm always going to be there when he needs me."

Ruth said, "Must have been the scarlet fever he had when he was a boy. I hear tell that can ruin a man for good."

"Hush, I hear him coming," Norma whispered.

Ruth and Robbye glanced at each other, knowing that this family secret was never to be mentioned.

Clyde walked into the kitchen, reached for a glass and quickly poured a two finger shot of bourbon. He took a quick sip and said, "Ladies, I think we need to do some visitin' first thing 'morrow morning. I'm meeting Ben and that ass of a doctor that came to town. Robbye, you and Ruth need to go see the young gal in the clinic."

Robbye said, "Her name is Nell and her baby boy is named Robert. Told me later she wanted a name from our family. I thought it was sweet naming him after my daddy. But if this ain't the damndest business. Now what's happened?"

"Seems as though our good friend the new doc from Mississippi called the State Welfare Agency with some cockeyed story about you and Ruth locking the girl up all day and using her as if she was your slave. That she worked for you and never got paid or helped with her baby. According to the new doc, you two were the cause of all the girl's trouble."

Clyde grinned as he told them the news; he liked winding his older sister, Ruth, into a downright frenzy of anger.

Ruth turned purple with rage, "That no-ccunt sumbitch! He's lying. Robbye, you and I best have a talk with Nell. 7:30 right, Clyde?"

"Yep. The Bird will be runnin' so get cleaned up, get some sleep; get ready for an early ride," said Clyde.

"Ain't nobody cared for that young girl more than us," Robbye said.

"We best sort this out nice and easy; tender spots all over this cat," said Clyde.

"Anyone want more to eat or drink? Times pushing fast," asked Norma.

"Is there a thigh in that bucket?" Robbye asked.

"Yep, here ya go, last one," said Norma handing Robbye the chicken thigh.

Robbye had the last drink from the Old Grandad, and they all headed for bed. 4:30am would come early.

Indeed 4:30am did come earlier than usual, or so it seemed. No one had a decent sleep. Clyde sternly said to all before they hit the road, "Simply tell the truth." By 6:00am, they were all loaded in Clyde's car heading for Jackson Landing.

First, they went to the clinic at 7:00 where Robbye and Ruth talked to Nell, then at 7:30, they pulled up to the old parish Courthouse, built in 1836. The sheriff's office was attached to the old courthouse. For some reason, it had been built with red brick.

It was a simple square structure that paled in comparison with the massive courthouse building and its huge columns. The requisite statue, dedicated to the men from Jackson Landing who never came back from the Civil War, dominated the entry. Everyone got out of the car as Ruth complained, "Damn waste of time," as they followed Clyde into the sheriff's office.

With a broad smile, Clyde said, "Ben, Melvin, what's up, boys? You got some questions to ask me and the ladies? Y'all all know my family?"

"Why yes, of course," they said as they all stood up.

"Ruth, Robbye, Norma, how y'all this morning? Can I get y'all some coffee? Mighty strong but good flavor," Ben said as he shook everyone's hand.

To which Clyde replied, "Well, then let's all go hear what the doc says and what the girl says. And I'm telling you up front, Melvin, if the stories don't match up, I'm gonna beat that sawbones bastard all the way to the Louisiana line. I'm not fooling with no man that lies 'bout my family."

Sheriff Ben laughed as he said, "Let's get to goin'. I ain't seen Clyde whoopin' someone's ass in a while now."

The whole group got in their separate cars and drove to the clinic. At the clinic, they got out and walked inside with State Trouper Melvin leading the way. Melvin asked the receptionist at the front desk if Doctor Montgomery was in his office.

The lady replied, "No, Doctor Montgomery and his staff had a special appointment north of town, 'bout three mile over the Mississippi state line."

"Well, how about his ambulance driver and his nurse?" Melvin inquired. "They all went with him. Said it was a special type emergency and they may be gone for a good while," the receptionist answered.

The sheriff started laughing, "Hell, Clyde, you scared the sawbones right out of the state!"

"Good riddance to Mississippi trash," said Ruth as she rolled her eyes. "Now, ladies, let's all get to work. And, Melvin, I think you've got enough information for a report. Right?"

"Yes, Ms. Ruth, I think I do," replied Melvin tipping his hat to her.

And with that, they went back to their cars, except Clyde and Norma who stayed and asked where Nell was. The receptionist said, "She's in the back of the clinic. That's where Doctor Montgomery told me to put her before he left town on his emergency."

Norma and Clyde walked down the dark hallway to an open room. The heat in the clinic was oppressive. There was no one else in the old building except Nell who was lying in the bed with no sheets, dressed in a dirty hospital gown with little Robert by her side breastfeeding.

Clyde looked away but Norma walked over and said, "Are you alright, dear?"

Nell replied, "I'm poorly parched as can be. I ain't had no water all mornin'."

Norma found a water pitcher and gave her a long steady drink, holding the whole pitcher to her lips. "What's your name, child?" Norma asked.

"Ize name Nell, and this here be Robert, my onliest child."

"We're gonna get you out of here and take you where you can get some care." Norma asked Nell. "Is that alright with you?"

"Yes, I s'pect so cuz I got nothing here to help me. I needs somethin' more for my baby. Ize ready to go anytime and be any place but here to get help."

Clyde walked over and said to Norma, "I'll go find a wheel chair."

He walked to the desk and asked the receptionist for a wheel chair to help Nell leave the clinic. The lady politely said, "Yessir, Mr. Fitzhugh. I'll bring it right out."

And with that simple kind gesture, life changed forever for Nell and little Robert, and also for Clyde and Norma. As Clyde helped Nell into the wheelchair, Norma whispered to him, "I think the Lord hears us, Clyde. I think the Lord knows that we try and be good people. He feels us. He feels our souls pleading for forgiveness."

Clyde simply nodded as they both walked behind the wheelchair helping Nell and Robert into the sunlight of a new day;, a new beginning and a new life.

Clyde sat easy in his rocking chair on the front porch of the Big House. It was a hot Saturday afternoon. The Louisiana humidity took your breath away. Leaves hung as if the trees were giving up to the heat of a summer Saturday afternoon.

A large glass of tea eased Clyde's comfort as he leaned back in his rocking chair on the front porch and watched the Cleveland Indians play his favorite team, the New York Yankees, on TV. The small black and white TV sat on an old wooden box.

Rabbit-ear antennas wrapped in aluminum foil, supposedly for better reception, stood out in different and odd angles. An extension cord ran across the porch through an open window to a newly installed electric plug.

Clyde watched with wonder at the little black and white TV. He thought it was the damndest thing he'd ever seen since the talkie thing. Watching the Yankees play was an experience too great to explain.

He was describing the dynamics of each play to Norma, sitting silently in her rocker. She had that longing summer stupor gaze while staring at the heat waves rising off the blacktop road. Every now and then she would comment 'oh yeah' or 'there they go'.

She had no concern or care what Tito Francona had just done or if the Yankees might bring in some person

Clyde referred to as the 'fireman or leave Whitey in to finish 'em off'. She drank her iced tea and waited for the heat to dissolve with the sunset.

Without so much as a twist of her head, Norma said, "Well, lookee who's riding a mule up to the front gate. Moses, what are you doing out in the heat of this scorcher of a day?"

Moses road on up to the fence, got off his mule and tied the reins to an oak tree. Clyde turned away from the TV and said, "Hey, Moses, come on over here and have a glass of iced tea, cold and sweet."

Moses came through the rickety gate and carefully sat down at the top of the stairs. "Why, thank you, Mr. Clyde, and, Ms. Norma. I s'pect I will. With such an invite, I'd be a fool to say no."

Norma got up and said, "I'll be right back with some iced tea."

"Well, neither teams been able to score yet but the Yankees are looking hot. Bottom of the 7th need something good to happen," said Clyde. "Moses, can you see the dang TV sitting where you be?"

"Why yassuh, Mister Clyde. I can see right well from where I be at. But thank you for askin'," replied Moses.

"Mickey Mantle be on deck, and I'm hopin' for the best. Got ten dollah on this game with Luke Faucheaux. Nothin' I like better than to win this bet," said Clyde as he anxiously watched the TV.

"Well, I s'pect ol Mr. Mantle may have somethin' to say. If you goin' to win, he be the one that make it so. He comin' up to bat yet?" Moses asked.

"He's on deck and looks like he's swinging good. By the way, Moses, what brings you down here on such a blistering hot day?" Clyde asked.

"Well, it be a long story. Shouldn't we wait for ol Mickey to show 'em how to play ball first? I be bettin' Mr. Faucheaux pacing the floor and prayin' hard," suggested Moses.

"Yep," Clyde said. "Mickey's steppin' up to the plate. Two outs. Man on first and second."

Mantle studied the pitcher, Mudcat Grant, a right hander who was throwing a pretty good ballgame. Mantle, a switch hitter, had been batting left-handed but switched to right for his last at bat. Mudcat took the signal and wound up throwing a 90-mile-an-hour fast ball in the strike zone, just on the right corner of home plate.

Mantle swung hard, spinning around as he connected dead center on the ball, driving it deep into left field. Francona backed up then watched as the ball flew well into the outfield bleachers.

Clyde jumped out of his rocking chair and let out a whoop as Norma pushed the screen door open. Clyde turned and said, "Norma, ol Mickey done won the game. Indians won't make it back in three more at bats. Whitey's got the ball moving today. And I'm gonna win ten dollahs."

All three of them anxiously watched the last three innings. The Yankees won 3 to 0. Things finally got quiet as Clyde got up and turned off the TV. In a more serious tone, he asked, "Ok, Moses, what's on your mind?"

Moses quietly said, "Mr. Clyde, I think we both feel betta talkin' on the back porch stead of out here in the front. Them young bucks passing be talkin' too much to the wrong folk…if you knows what I mean?"

Clyde looked at him sternly and said, "I'll meet you round back."

Clyde stood up and went to the screen door. Moses walked down the steps and began the long walk to the back of the house. Colored folk didn't walk through a white man's house, no matter the invite. A long, ugly understanding that seemed more traditional to both men.

Once to the back porch, Clyde said, "Come on up and take a load off a them shoes. Norma, would you please get Moses and me some more sweet tea, ma'am?"

Norma brought a pitcher of tea and said, "I'll step inside and let you men folk enjoy the evening air."

"How long we knew each other, Mr. Clyde? Nye on to 'bout forty years?" Moses asked.

"Yep," said Clyde. "I think we don knew each other since we were about 14." Clyde then added in a hushed tone, "If I remember exactly, we were both sweet on the same gal. Am I right about that, Moses?"

"Yassuh, I member it all too well. And we both knew where that all done went to," responded Moses.

Clyde laughed and said, "Deed, we do. But I want you to always member I never said no or yes 'bout our concerns. I did my best for all. *A life is a life, and we gots to protect it if we gonna have a future.*"

"That shor be true," said Moses.

"Now the past is gone; it's just us, so what be the word, Moses? What is it you want me to help with?"

Moses smiled and said, "Mr. Clyde you and your whole family been good to me and my kinfolk and I know it ain't been easy for a white man to be kind and help poor black folk like so many I know that been helped by the Fitzhugh family. Ya'll been the most honest, fairest folk I know to all who needed. Now my grandson gonna need extra special help and you the only friend I can ask to help him make something of his self in this white man's world. I cogitated on this a good while now and I'm leading up to a mighty big favor. But first what you think of me a asking?"

Clyde looked at Moses with his tough Irish face and quietly said, "Well Moses first nigh on to 30 years or more. Tell me something that be true. Now you tell me, and I'll see what I can do to help. That child that was born to that gal,LaTonya, when we was both young and hot-cattin' around. Was it yours for sure? You know we was both sweet on her."

Moses stared him straight on and said, "It be my child, Mr. Clyde. I swear it be me that bring that child. I knew you be sweet on her, but I just don out-foxed you."

Clyde laughed and laughed again. "I knew it! Somehow, I always knew it."

"You ol fox. But you know, Moses, in the world of our thoughts, it's the thought of love and friendship that matters most. And still we both loved our loves."

"No more true words be spoken," said Moses. "And I can only say thank you and God bless you for saving my boy from those terrible Klan men. They was about to lynch that boy till you stepped in."

"He was beat half to death, but you saved his life during that cruel, savage time. And it ain't ever gone be forgotten; nassuh, never."

Folding his arms behind his head, Clyde said, "Well, I never liked them secret society types. Too damn scared to show their no-count faces unless they got a poor soul they can whoop up on. I really despise those no count bastards."

Clyde went on, "Well, now what's all this business really about laying up here on the back porch a talking 'bout life and enjoying some tea?"

Moses laughed and said, "Mr. Clyde, that young girl, Nell, that you and I helped at that wreck and that young man who be my grandson, they needs some help."

"They's-a-talking 'bout gettin themselves married soon, and he be looking for more work. He works hard, be clean, tends to needs at the church and save money he earn. A fine youngun. I figured on that you may be a needing some hep soon. So, I think, if anyone can help this young man, it be you. I knew how well you treated that young man I brought into dis here world. And I knew you fought against them white men that be after him. God, help us all. And l's jest trying to help my grandson gets a little bit further along this tough ol road we say be life."

"Why I appreciate that thought, Moses, and God best know we all need help. But I really don't think I got enough work to be done to keep the boy busy. Ain't no one but me and Ms. Norma," said Clyde.

"Well, that be true, but I had to ask you man to man, Mr. Clyde, and I knows you will keep that thought in mind," Moses responded.

Clyde looked at his old, black friend who he knew had struggled in the white world just to survive. But a man, regardless of color who could always be counted on to help. A man Clyde trusted.

"I will, Moses. I promise I will. You're a black man in a white man's world but more importantly to me than color is that you are a true friend. I promise I'll do my best to help those young folk move ahead. We'll make something work for them, but only because you say he's a good boy becoming a good man. We clear 'bout that, Moses?"

"Yassuh, you gots my word, and that's the best I can do. That's all a man can ask for," Moses said, "care and friendship."

After Moses thanked Norma for the sweet tea, he and Clyde shook hands as they parted company that afternoon; both men still hoping that somehow, they would each do their small part and help others survive, maybe even thrive, in this world they both knew from experience was full of sorrow and hardship.

Two days later, on Monday, Norma told Clyde it was time to cut the grass and clean up. So, he got the old mower out from under the house and filled it full of gas, checked the oil and cleaned the spark plug. Finally, after pulling the starter cord 5-6 times, the old mower came to life.

He took off his work shirt and began to mow the grass around the dog pen. The mower was running just fine when Clyde felt an odd, sporadic pounding in his chest. He left the mower running and was walking to the back porch when he collapsed to his knees.

Grabbing his chest, he fell forward but caught himself with his left arm before he collapsed on the ground.

"Norma!" He yelled.

She walked out nonchalantly, but when she saw Clyde, she ran down the steps of the porch screaming, "Oh my God, what's happened?"

"Call the sheriff. 1 think I'm dying," gasped Clyde.

Norma ran to the telephone and cranked three times. Ms. Minnie was on phone duty, "Yes, Norma?"

"Minnie, I think Clyde's had a heart attack. Call the sheriff and tell him to send help," Norma pleaded.

"Oh, bless this new telephone thing. I'm callin' now," replied Minnie before quickly hanging up.

The deputy sheriff was near Greenwood when he got the call about Clyde. Siren blaring and lights blinking, he soon pulled in front of the Big House. Norma helped get Clyde to the car, and they sped off to the doctor in Angola.

The drive wasn't more than 20 minutes, but for Norma, it seemed like hours. Clyde remained conscious, but his chest felt like a boulder was lying on him. They made it to the small, but competent, hospital in Angola. The deputy had called ahead, and the emergency room staff met them at the entry.

They quickly put Clyde on a gurney and hooked up an IV as they push him to the emergency room. He looked up at Norma and said, "Did you turn the damn mower off?" Then chokingly laughed.

"Please lay still," instructed the nurse calmly.

Clyde ignored her and said to Norma, "Get a hold of Moses, and tell him we're gonna need the help."

Norma was confused by his request but simply said, "Yes, darlin'. Now try and relax."

Clyde was in the hospital for several weeks before the doctor said he could go home, but he was under strict orders to continue to rest. No heavy physical activities, no coffee and absolutely no alcohol. Clyde looked at the doctor and said, "Well, that's a hard task to follow, but hell, I'll try anything once."

The doctor laughed, "I know you will. But seriously, you had a heart attack. Not a major one but close. You're a lucky man, Clyde, so don't think you're indestructible. Take it slow and easy. Get your strength back. And take your medicine as directed. Promise?"

"You got my word, Doc; and I'll keep the volume down to a fever pitch."

They both laughed. "I'll see you in two weeks. You got a ride home?" The doctor asked.

"Yep, the prettiest gal you ever seen," said Clyde just as Norma walked into the room with a young black man and a wheel chair.

"Clyde, I'm here to fetch you, and I brought help. This young man goes by the name of Booty. Moses said he would give us all the help we need," said Norma as she helped Clyde to the edge of the bed. Clyde looked Booty up and down.

A strong good-looking young man with a bashful but full smile. Clyde reached out his hand and Booty did the same. They shook hands and held each other for just a moment testing each other's strength. It was the manly thing to do, and Clyde liked the feel that Booty's touch conveyed.

Booty and the nurse helped Clyde into the wheel chair and gathered all his belongings, including a bag full of medicine. Clyde turned to Booty, looking him up and down again, and said, "Well, what the hell you lookin' at? Get me outa this place. We got work to do."

That's how Booty came in to Clyde's life, and over the years, he became the son Clyde never had.

The first month of Clyde at home passed quickly.

As any other typical early morning, Norma stood at her stove, adjusted the heat to low on the cast-iron skillet as she turned the buttered fried bread before putting it on a plate. "Clyde," she called as she placed a cup of chickory coffee next to the plate. "Breakfast is ready. How you doin' in there?"

"Happier than a puppy with two peckers," he yelled back.

"Don't get smart with me, Clyde. Booty will be here soon. Hell, here he is now," she said as she watched him make his way to the back porch. "Good morning, Booty. You hungry or need some coffee?"

Booty was standing outside the kitchen door, as black hired help wasn't allowed in the kitchen unless they were cooking or cleaning. Another ugly tradition that lingered.

"Ms. Norma, I be steppin' high today. Best gimme some of your special coffee please, ma'am," replied Booty.

Clyde strolled in to the kitchen and Norma said to him, "Why not you take your plate out on the porch with Booty? I've got to get going to work. And you need to let Booty know 'bout Tommy comin' over here after noon."

"I s'pect I will. Best idea I've had this mornin'," Clyde said smiling as he got up and moved to the back porch screen door.

He knew what was coming next as he heard Norma reply, "The best idea you've had is gettin' your sorry ass out that bed."

Clyde laughed hard and said to Booty, "Well, come on sit down, and let's watch Son shave his ugly face."

"Yassuh, Mista Clyde, don't mind if I do since you be asking'," said Booty as he moved to the chair next to Clyde and carefully sat down.

Clyde grinned, looking at Booty and said, "Well then, have a seat, Mr. Smartass."

Booty looked startled and quickly said, "Why, Mista Clyde, I'm just trying to be talking. You knows I be trying."

Clyde laughed his deep laugh and looked sternly at Booty before breaking into another laugh and said, "Gotcha, didn't I? Ooowhee! I done scared you pale."

It took a moment before Booty realized this was one of Clyde's never-ending jokes. He wasn't sure how to act next when Clyde reached out, touched his forearm and said, "Booty, today you're gonna meet my nephew. Actually, my great nephew, Robbye May's nephew to be exact. He's coming from Jackson Landing to spend some time with us. Now what do you think 'bout that?"

Booty wasn't sure about this news. His first thought was that he was out the door and a new replacement was coming for a few weeks. Which to him meant no money for a while. Knowing full well he had Booty shook up, Clyde kept stirring the gossip pot.

"Yeah, he's a young boy, 'bout a year younger than you, Booty. Supposed to be a good worker. Tough as a boot. Drive nails with his fist. Chop firewood afore the tree falls. And likes dogs, which we both know you don't like. Right?" Clyde said hoping that Booty would take the bait.

Booty bit on the hook of Clyde's line, "Why I does all them things now, Mista Clyde, ceppin' too much dealing with them hounds, specially that Catahoula."

Clyde knew he had pushed the boy far enough. He relented and said in a quiet voice, "I know that. You think I'm going to have that boy, who probably can't find his ass with both hands, come over here and do your job? Why, hell fire, I don't know how we would have survived without you this last month."

"What's more, I want you to get to know this boy. I want you to teach him about the ways and works of a Louisiana country town. Teach him how to work and how hard it is to spend your life living day by day. You and him can split up the work get it done and go exploring."

"Berries be comin' in, and I know those girls up the road livin' with Aunt Sue will be out pickin'. Your grandpa Moses said you had a hankering for one of them gals? Ain't that right, Norma?"

Norma opened the screen door gave Clyde and Booty cups of coffee and split another piece of fried bread in half and placed it on the small plate between them. Norma replied as she smiled, "Why everybody who knows Booty knows he's got a sweet tooth for a special girl who happens to have a son named after Sister's daddy."

Booty smiled, which triggered another big laugh from Clyde. "I gotcha! Gotcha again," Clyde said with a big laugh, "HA."

Finally understanding they were joking with him and not at him, Booty said, "Yassuh, you had ol Booty bit worried and a thinkin' 'bout my gal. Her name be Nell.

You the one done save her life, Mr. Clyde, and for that, Booty thanks you very much. Yassuh, very much."

"I know," Clyde said smiling. "Your Grandpa Moses told me all about your gal. Now drink that coffee and eat some bread. The Son show's 'bout to start."

They both looked out to the south as Son walked out on his back porch for his morning ritual. Clyde and Booty hooted with laughter until the show was over.

Clyde turned serious as he told Booty the chores he needed to be done that day. He finished Booty's work schedule with a final strongly worded, "I want everything cleaned up real good and neat around the house. You best get to cracken cause your new work buddy will be here after dinner."

My name is Tommy. Clyde Fitzhugh was my great uncle. My life was different than most of the white kids I knew. My father was a military man, and our family moved often. Often is really not the best description; by the time I was 23, we had moved 29 times.

Chasing my father's military career was defined by exceptionalism and determination – not just for him but the entire family.

As a young kid, when summer rolled around and if we weren't moving, I would spend the fleeting three months of summer and no responsibility with my relatives in Louisiana. I loved the hot, humid summers and my relatives, who made me feel like a grown man.

Coffee in the mornings, thick and dark with a dollop of brandy or bourbon was exactly what a 13-year-old boy needed before the first Lucky Strike of the day. I was happy to be considered an adult, especially with little, if any, adult supervision.

My older brother, Will, was with me. He had his own ways but didn't quite have the inquisitive wild streak that ran through my young body. But what a wonderful way to face the rigors of doing nothing by running wild wide open?

Occasionally, boredom reared its black dog head. Usually after the second week, and during that time, the anxiety of life would start to haunt me until I could discover some new outlandish adventure. However, this particular summer was going to be different.

I was going to visit my uncles in a busted railroad town about twenty miles from Jackson Landing and stay as long as I wanted. My older brother, Will, decided to stay at the French House, as we called my grandmother's country home. But my brother, Will, as usual, had found a summer sweetheart he met at the local 'malt shop'.

He figured chasing her was better than running wild in the likes of a broken-down Louisiana town. But me? I never looked back as soon I was riding out of Jackson Landing to the rough and tumble of Greenwood.

In past years, I always stayed with my aunt Robbye. She lived with her mother and my grandmother's sister, Ruth. They were mainstays in the political and cultural life of the small town of the 'Landing', as locals referred to Jackson Landing.

Robbye was the director of the local State Welfare office, and Ruth worked as the senior secretary for the parish sheriff, Ben Cummings. Robbye and Ruth had been employed by some local, state or federal government agency for as long as I could remember.

They lived on the outskirts of the Landing in a long, one-story house. All the rooms opened to a screened-in porch that ran the length of the house. The continued open air and the continuous whirling ceiling fans provided a tolerable temperature and cooling breeze.

We called it the French House because each bedroom had large French doors opening to a screened in porch that ran the length of the house. The large living area in the middle was perfect for parties, which seemed continuous during the summer months.

Guests were mainly local politicos from the area, an occasional Congressman, retired Governors or just friends of friends. The parties were quite the deal. A lot of drinking, great southern food, congenial friendship with a dash of politics.

The property itself was beautiful. An abundance of huge oak trees with wisps of Spanish moss, weeping willows, cherry trees, ligustrums, wild tallows, all providing cooling shade from the summer heat.

A driveway bordered with oleanders and crepe myrtles, circled from the front of the house and flowed down to a large pond well stocked with crappie, bream and the biggest catfish I ever caught. Fishing the pond was a wonderful way to spend a lazy afternoon.

My aunt Robbye's 1956 Ford with 'three on the tree' was at Will and my beck and call. We drove that car over the dirt roads, mimicking scenes from the movie *Thunder Road*. Hell, I could barely see over the steering wheel. Regardless, I could handle any tricky corner by doing a decent power slide and down shifting to second to force the turn at a pretty good speed.

Occasionally, to spice things up, one of us would climb on the roof or the trunk of the car while the driver would swerve and turn trying to throw the rider off. We both got thrown several times.

Fortunately for us, we ended our wild stunts with just scrapes and several ugly gravel burns. But we would laugh until our sides hurt at whomever got 'chunked', as we called it. Those wild rides were our great escape from the tedium of occasional nothingness.

This particular summer, my older brother, Will, decided he wanted to stay for a longer visit. Will and I got along pretty well until the boredom of three older women would drive one of us up a wall. Will had grown used to the daily ritual of reading, napping or driving the old Ford plus a wild and fun loving girlfriend.

He was college bound and I guess needed some better looking companions than me.

But me, it was all about time for fun and antics of my uncles in Greenwood.

The scent of serious country living, with new and very different people, would forever draw me to interesting, and at times dangerous, experiences. At my uncles' homes, I could really be me, no questions asked. As long as I stayed out of serious trouble I was accepted and offered almost total freedom.

Rolling my own cigarettes? No problem. A secret sip of Old Grandad in my morning coffee? Simply a good way to start the day.

My uncles and aunts in Greenwood called me Tommy rather than Tom, but regardless I always answered 'yessir' or 'yes mam'.

My uncle Clyde and his wife, Norma, said I could come visit for a while, but I always wanted to stay as long as possible. I asked Robbye if she would call Uncle Clyde and ask if I could stay a week or two longer.

Clyde answered her call and said, "Why sure. Besides, I got somebody I want Tommy to meet. How old is that boy now?"

Aunt Robbye replied, "Why, I think he's 13 going on 21."

"Perfect," said Uncle Clyde. "I'll be over this afternoon to pick him up."

I could hardly wait. I packed my personal belongings, stepped out onto the long screened-in porch and lit a cigarette. As I stood looking out at the trees, I remembered the time the year before as if it were yesterday when Nell with her baby came running though the oleanders begging for help.

What a time that was, Aunt Ruth with her pistol and Will with my dad's rifle. Man, that was some kinda excitement, which had really scared me. I'd never seen a grown man like old Watson seriously threaten anyone, much less Will and me.

What a strange coincidence that my uncle Clyde had been the one to rescue Nell after damned Watson had nearly killed her on his nightmarish last ride to eternity.

I was just taking the last drag of my cigarette when Uncle Clyde pulled into the drive in his new yellow Buick Skylark. I noticed there was a colored boy sitting next to him in the front seat. Clyde got out of the car and walked toward the house.

Aunt Robbye had joined me on the front porch for a quick smoke, and we both watched as he sauntered up. He stopped, looked at me and said, "Boy, get over here, and let me have a good look at you."

I hustled over, and Uncle Clyde wrapped his arms around me and said, "Why you're on your way to bein' a man. What do you think of my new hot rod?" He asked as he and Robbye both laughed.

"She's a real beauty. I'll bet she'll really fly," I said.

"Yep," Clyde said. "That's why I call her the Bird. And I'm gonna let you drive her soon as I check you out."

With that promise, I reached up and gave him a big hug and looked straight at the car and at the colored boy in the front seat. He had a serious look on his face. His eyes were wide and frightened. Clyde turned to the car and yelled, "Booty, get your ass out the car and come over here."

The boy opened the door, got out and slowly walked over. He looked at the ground as he walked. "Why, Booty, you're looking better every time I see you. Just look at you being a fine young man," Aunt Robbye said.

Booty looked up and smiled, "Thank you, Ms. Robbye. Those be kind words."

"You sure look bigger and better than you did when I saw you out at Mam's house. How long were you there?" Aunt Robbye asked.

Booty replied, "Bout a year or more. I kinda forgets."

"I know," responded Aunt Robbye. "Those were some difficult times for you. Tryin' to grow up with all the other children. But Lord, you have made a fine looking young man."

"Come on over here, boy, and meet your new partner," said Uncle Clyde as he gestured toward us.

Booty moved with a shuffle toward me and then just stood there looking at the ground. Looking at me, Uncle Clyde said, "Tommy, this here's Booty. He works for me and helps Norma when she needs some helping hands. He lives up the road from us with Aunt Sue and a bunch of young girls. Booty will tell you that story later."

Then, looking at Booty, he said, "Booty, this here's Tommy. You're gonna show him how a city slicker like him can learn to love this place. You boys happy with this arrangement?"

"Yassuh, Mister Clyde, I be happy to know this boy," said Booty as he thrust out his hand.

I reached for his hand shook it. Booty smiled. We stood there for a moment until Clyde said, "Alright, you two, get in the car, and let's get out of here afore Robbye starts to blubberin'. Both ya'll hop in the back."

"Heading home?" Robbye asked anxiously.

To which Clyde replied, "Nope, heading north."

With that, he waved and sped west toward Greenwood.

Speeding ain't in it I thought as Clyde roared down the dirt road leading to the highway to Greenwood. Booty didn't say a word. Me? I was scared as hell. Clyde had the Yellow Bird going 50, maybe 60, miles per hour, sliding through corners and damn near airborne over lifts in the road.

It was a real joy ride. Finally, we reached the highway and headed north. Coming to the turn to Greenwood, Clyde was doing about 75, and we quickly passed the small town. I spoke up and asked, "Whereabouts are we going, Uncle Clyde?"

He smiled and looked at me in the rearview mirror and said, "Hamburgers. Best in this part of Louisiana, and I'm thirsty."

Well, that did me in. I looked at Booty, and he gave a sheepish grin as he shrugged his shoulders. Soon enough, we were slowing down and pulled into a dirt parking lot outside a small clapboard building with the word

'Restaurant' painted on a big sign over the door. Clyde stopped the car turned to us and asked, "What you boys want, hamburgers or cheeseburgers?"

We both replied, "Cheeseburgers and French fries.'

"Alright, and to drink, I'll get two R.C. Colas and something special to top my day off," said Clyde.

He got out of the car and walked toward the store. I turned to Booty and said, "You get to do this often?"

He stammered and said, "Nosuh, Mister Tommy"

"Tommy is fine with me, and please, Booty, no more of that 'yassuh, nosuh' shit. We got to get along, and I'm here to have fun. So, let's get that straight ok?" We sat in the backseat sweating in the Louisiana sun anxiously waiting to see Uncle Clyde coming, hopefully he hadn't drunk too much.

Booty looked at me and laughed, "Alright, Tommy! Now look out here come the man and he's walking tall and proud. We good."

Clyde was carrying a paper bag obviously full of food. Hunger jumped on me as he handed the bag to us and said, "No eatin', boys; we got one more stop."

"Did you get your top-of-the-day drink?" I asked as I secured the bag between Booty and me.

"Why hell yeah, I got me a Grapette, and one of those cheeseburgers is mine," Clyde replied as he started the car.

I looked in the bag, and sure enough, there was a Grapette and three huge cheeseburgers and loads of fries. He handed us the R. C. Colas and said, "No drinking till we gets where we're a goin'."

We tore out of the driveway like we'd robbed a bank. We drove about four miles before turning down a dirt road heading into the woods. I looked at Booty, and he just shrugged and turned his hands up as if to say, 'I don't have any idea'.

It wasn't long until we came to a big open field. There were people scattered all over, but their cars were all neatly parked between two 50-gallon drums holding up long stretches of rope. Then I saw a big baseball backstop and men, or older boys, strolling around the field throwing a baseball to each other and taking turns swinging bats.

A BASEBALL FIELD in the middle of nowhere. I was in awe. How could this have happened and how did Uncle Clyde know about all of this?

Clyde parked his car at the end of a set of wooden bleachers. We all got out and he said, "Gimme my cheeseburger and Grapette, and you boys dig in."

While Booty and I got our cheeseburgers and fries, Clyde opened the trunk of the car and was getting something, and was putting it on. He walked around to the front of the car with a big chest protector on and a catcher's face mask balanced on the top of his head. Eating away at his cheeseburger he said, "Ya'll enjoy the game."

Then, as he walked out onto the field, everyone was yelling, as the teams went to their respective wooden dugouts. Then all got a little quiet. Clyde finished his cheeseburger and chugged down his Grapette. Throwing the paper napkins and bottle in the trash, he turned to the large crowd that had gathered and yelled, "Everybody ready for some red-hot baseball?"

The crowd whooped and stomped. Cries of 'let's go' and 'hell yes' echoed across the field into the woods.

What surprised me was everyone had been waiting for Clyde to show up. He was the umpire. Not just the only umpire but the only umpire the teams could agree on. He was the man they both trusted as fair to all. Never in my life did I see such a remarkable sight as I did that day.

The only man these people, these players, trusted to be fair and impartial was my uncle Clyde. Man oh man was I proud to be his kinfolk.

Booty and I sat on the hood of the Bird, ate our cheeseburgers and drank our R.C. Colas. We were having a swell time as the innings flew by. But around the 5th inning, with Northwood Tigers in the lead over the Greenwood Foxes by one run, I noticed a man in the bleachers next to our car pointing at us and making what looked like snide remarks to his girlfriend.

And then I heard the words, "Hey, nigger, what you think you're doin here? This be a white-folk game."

Neither Booty or I moved or looked his way. Again, this time as a shout, he yelled, "Nigger, you betta get your ass out of here, boy, or I'm gonna kick that black ass till you can't walk. You hear me, boy?"

At this shout, Clyde looked our way. He stopped the game took his catcher's mask off and walked over to the car. He looked at us and shouted as he pointed at the man, "Is that piss-ant redneck, peckerwood bothering you boys?"

We both said, "No, sir. No one's bothering us."

Clyde said slowly, but very loud, "Well, that son-of-a-bitch is bothering me."

He turned and looked right at the man and said, "You got somethin' to say to my boys? Let's hear it, big dog, or get back on the porch."

The man stood up and looked at Clyde, "Do you know who I am?"

Clyde looked at him and laughed as he started to walk toward the wooden bleacher and said, "Why, hell yeah I know who you are; you're the dumb son-of-a- bitch that's botherin' me. So, are you gonna shut your mouth or keep botherin' me?"

"Well, we'll just have to see 'bout that, won't we?" Was all the younger man said.

With that said, Clyde walked back out to the field to the pitcher's mound and motioned for both coaches to come out. Both men walked slow, but determinedly, toward the mound. When they reached the mound, the coach from Northwood, Rooster McManus, aptly nicknamed for his red hair, asked, "Ok, Clyde; what's the problem?"

Clyde pointed at the man in the bleachers and said, "See that peckerwood over there? I can't place his name, but he was yellin' at my boys sittin' on the front of my car." Clyde then slyly said, "Rooster, he's botherin' me so much, I can hardly tell a ball from a strike when your boys are at bat."

"That so?" Rooster said. "What can I do to help your eyesight?"

"Well, you can either throw him out of here, or get him to apologize to my boys and shut his goddamn mouth," Clyde said loud and sternly.

"And if I don't?" Rooster asked.

"I'll have to tell the league commissioner that you forfeited the game," said Clyde, now looking at Leon Laster, the coach for Greenwood.

Rooster and Leon both spoke at once. "Now come on, Clyde. You know we'll have nothing but trouble from that bastard. He's Klan," Rooster said loud enough for all to hear.

"I know damn well who and what he is, but ain't no son-of-a-bitch gonna call my boy a nigger. So, make up your minds, and I'll back you no matter what. We clear?" he demanded.

They both nodded yes, and all three started walking toward the man. They stood together and called him out. He got up slowly and made his way to the field. Rooster spoke first, "Henry, what in the hell are you doing at a ballgame calling someone a nigger?"

Henry Franklin knew what he was and what he'd done and said, "Well, I call it liken I sees it, and if ya'll don't like it, you can stick it where the sun don't shine."

Clyde looked down at him, Henry being shorter, and said, "You called my boy a nigger; now you're gonna apologize nice and quiet like, or I'm forcing a forfeit of this game. And I sure as hell will let it be known to all in Northwood, you and your smart-ass mouth were the cause."

"You can't get away with that," Henry threatened.

To which Clyde replied, "The hell I can't, and if you don't stop mouthing off to me, I'm going to beat your sorry ass to a pulp right here and right now in front of all these folks. Then when I'm finished kickin your sorry ass all over this field, I'm gonna tell the folks from Northwood that you caused the forfeit and game over – Greenwood wins, and you're the one that cost the team the game. So, what's it gonna be?"

Henry stammered and said, "I ain't gonna forget this, Clyde. And I'm gonna let my brother, Johnnie, know what you done."

Clyde laughed and laughed hard. "Why you do that, you little shit. You tell that goddamn brother of yours I said his wife's so damn ugly, she'd break a mirror, and his dogs can't hunt cuz they're no good biscuit-eatin' whore dogs."

"Now, Henry, you repeat to me what I just asked you to say then, walk over there and apologize to them two boys. Real nice like, cuz I'm tired of talking to your dumbass. You walkin', or am I callin' the game?"

Henry scowled and said, "I ain't none too pleased with how I been treated, and I sure nuff gon talk to Johnnie."

With that, he repeated to Clyde what Clyde had said. Then he turned and walked over to me and Booty. He looked straight at us and said, "I apologize for what I said."

Clyde then said in a loud voice, "And you ain't gonna do that again. Right, Henry?"

Henry mumbled, "I ain't never gonna say that to you again." He turned to Clyde and said, "Ok?"

Clyde looked at him, turned and yelled, "Play ball."

Henry climbed back up the bleachers. Booty and I ate our cheeseburgers, drank our R.C. Colas and watched Greenwood beat the hell out of Northwood, 8 to 2. Hot damn, we were we excited!

Clyde calmly walked off the field to the car. He opened the trunk, threw in his mask and chest protector, closed the trunk and said, "Let's roll, boys."

As we slowly made our way to the main road, the Greenwood fans, and some of the Northwood people, were yelling, 'Hey, Clyde' or 'Good calls behind the plate'.

I didn't hear one comment about the Henry fiasco, just a heck of a lot of compliments and good-natured fist pumps.

It was at that moment, I realized how well respected and trusted my uncle Clyde was throughout the parish. The crowd waited for him to show up, then backed him up when he backed down a member of the Klan and then applauded him after the game. I was some kind of proud.

We were roaring along at 70 mph and Clyde said, "You boys enjoy the game?"

Booty replied, "Yassuh; we sure nuff did."

"And, Tommy, what did you make of the game?" He asked.

"It was really something. Uncle Clyde, I swear I've never had such an excitin' time. This is a day I'll always remember. That be sure," I replied.

"Well," Clyde said, "least we got him talking like a redneck. Right, Booty?"

Booty laughed, "Yassuh, yassuh; he be soundin' even better once we get to berry pickin'."

Then they both laughed and laughed as I sat and wondered what the hell they were talking about. I was soon to find out.

Before we reached the Big House, Clyde brought up an issue about the hounds. I noticed Booty, who was sitting in the back, hunkered up and got real nervous. You could hear his voice slightly quiver as he quietly asked, "What that be 'bout, Mr. Clyde?"

"Booty, that durn Catahoula named Toto done got up under the house and had that litter of pups she been carryin'. We gonna have to get her distracted like and crawl under the house and get them pups. She's hungry and I think she already ate one of them."

I sat stone still and asked, "What you mean she ate one?"

Clyde said determinedly, "When a bitch dog get real hungry and realize that one of their pups ain't doing well or has outright died, they often eat the dead or dying pup. It ain't purty, but it's part of runnin' a bunch of hounds. Ain't that right, Booty?"

"Yassuh, Mister Clyde. You be speakin' true 'bout that. But who gonna do the distractin' and who gonna do the gettin'?"

"Why I s'pect you and Tommy best decide that. And while you be figuring, figure out the distractin' first. Then let me know before we get to the house," said Clyde.

Clyde put on the brakes and turned into the diner where we got the cheeseburgers. "You boys want something to drink or eat?"

"I'll take a Coke Cola," said Booty.

"Make that two," I said. Thinking about them puppies and that Catahoula made my stomach a little queasy.

Clyde hopped out of the car and walked into the diner. Booty and I looked at each other in a bit of a shock. Finally, Booty said, "Tommy, you ever done this afore?"

"Nope, I never even heard about it afore now. You sure Clyde's not foolin' with us?" I responded.

"Nahsuh, Nahsuh," Booty said. "I done seen this happen to other hounds, and it ain't no easy thing to work on."

"Well, what you think we should do?" I asked, wondering if it was better to do the distracting or the getting.

"I think I'll do the grabbin', whilst you does the distractin'. Sound alright to you, Tommy?" Booty said.

"Well, I don't know nothin' 'bout either one. What'd I gotta do to distract?" I hesitantly asked.

Booty replied, "Well, best thing is we gets a big ham bone with plenty of meat still on that bone. Ties it up to a rope and you throw it to the bitch. As she comes to the meat, you keep pullin' it away till you can grab her collar and hang on."

"You best hang on cause whilst you do that, I be crawlin' with a box to put them puppies inside then get the heck out from under that house fast as I can."

"Sounds like a good plan to me," I said. "But what if the dog let's go of that bone and goes back to them pups?"

"Well there, ol Booty will be in a heap of trouble, so you best make sure that hound loves that bone meat. You know folks say, 'The closer to the bone, the sweeter the meat'. So, we gots to have a good, meaty bone. That be Booty's scape," he said.

The door to the diner opened, and Clyde walked out all wobbly legged holding a big paper sack in his hands. I figured he'd had a couple of big drinks and couldn't drive.

He walked up to the car and said in a slur, "Tommy I'm mighty tired. You drive us home, whilst I take a snooze in the back seat. Move over, Booty; I'm coming in."

"But I'm not good at driving, Uncle Clyde"

He replied, "Well, damn time you figured it out. Now let's roll. I'm tired after all that hoop de do at the ball game."

With that, he gave the paper bag to Booty, got in back seat, laid back and immediately started snoring. Booty reached in the bag and pulled out the Coke Colas. While he opened the bottles, I started the car, backed up and pulled out onto the highway heading for Greenwood.

I figured out the gears with a grind here and there and soon the little Bird was flying down the road with me steering like there was no tomorrow, so much power in a little car. I was doing 60 mph, and there was plenty of horsepower which I figured I might eventually need.

Booty sat quietly in the back. I think my driving scared the hell out of him. Clyde snored with occasional incoherent mumbles. Soon, the turn off to Greenwood was upon us, and I slowed and down shifted to second gear as I turned the corner. Learning to drive in Aunt Robbye's old stick shift Ford came in mighty handy that day.

We pulled up to the Big House and Clyde woke up smiling, "Booty, get me another drink out of that bag."

Booty reached in and surprisingly pulled out a Grapette instead of a pint of whiskey. Clyde took a big gulp and said, "Damn things always make me sleepy. Keep digging, boy."

Booty reached in the bag again, and this time, he pulled out the biggest ham bone I had ever seen.

"Here's your distraction, Tommy," he said, as if he knew all along what we had been thinking.

"You boys see if you can get that hound to eat some dog chow. I'm mighty durn tired and we'll get them pups early tomorrow morning. That big hambone should get her morning appetite moving. What you boys think of that?"

Booty and I both let out a sigh as I said, "I think that's the best idea I've had all day."

Clyde laughed and told Booty, "You go on up to Aunt Sue's and we'll see you first thing in the morning. Gotta start early, we don't want to miss Son's shaving lesson."

We all laughed. Booty took off and I was pretty worn. I went to bed that night full of cheeseburgers, fries and a big R.C. I knew the morning would come soon and the excitement would start at day break.

I slept very sound with a stand up fan blowing a gentle breeze across the room. The windows were open and the sound of crickets helped calm my overly excited mind.

"Time to get up, boy. Coffees on the stove and Norma's making you a special breakfast. Biscuits and sawmill gravy. That should stand you up. We got a lot to do this morning. Booty will be here in about half an hour. So up ya go."

I dragged myself out of a deep sleep and a comfortable bed. Got dressed, cleaned up and headed toward the kitchen. Norma had breakfast on the table just as the sun was coming up. Clyde poured me a cup of coffee.

I took a sip and looked at him. He winked at me knowing I tasted a touch of whiskey in my cup. Norma was facing her stove as Clyde lifted his finger to his lips indicating our morning secret.

There was a scratching sound on the screen door to the back porch and Norma said, "C'mon in, Booty. Chickory coffee and biscuits."

Booty came inside the kitchen and eased into a chair next to me and said, "Mornin," to everyone.

Clyde said, "You boys eat up we've got to get those puppies sooner than later."

We both replied, "Yassuh" at the same time and started laughing. Clyde smiled as a caring parent would to their child. It made me feel so good. Especially sitting with Booty in the kitchen of the Big House. We gobbled down the biscuits and drank the coffee. We were ready.

"Alright, let's get going. Tommy grab that sack over there next to Norma. That's the hambone. We'll get some rope from the dog pen. Booty, you got a box for them little monsters?"

"Yassuh, Mr. Clyde, I'm ready to get them pups"

We stood up from the table and walked out to the back porch. Got the hambone and Booty got a good rope from the dog pen. I tied the hambone on and Booty moved to the side of the house to sneak in and get the puppies while I was to lure the Catahoula to the other side after the bone.

Clyde had a powerful flashlight he shone under the house and finally pinpointed the Catahoula and her pups. She snarled at the intrusion. I thought, *Man, this is gonna get real exciting in about 10 minutes.*

Clyde checked the rope on the meaty hambone and said, "Now, Tommy, you gotta throw that bone close but not to close. She's gotta get a good smell of that meat.

She'll slowly slink toward the bait, and you have to pull nice and slow toward the side of the house. Can you handle this?"

"Yep, I can do this," I replied in my most confident-sounding voice.

I kneeled down, looking straight at the dog and her mewling puppies. I had the bone in hand and tossed it about two feet from the dog. She began sniffing the air and slowly got to her feet. Scruffy mean didn't do her justice, she was fierce looking.

She was snapping at the air and slowly pursuing the bone as I drug it toward me and Clyde. But here's the thing, Clyde didn't tell me what I should do when the hound reached the edge of the house, and this menacing animal was coming straight toward me. I backed up a little and pulled the bone a little too fast. "Slow up a bit," Clyde said.

The dog jumped. I pulled the bone away from her, but she kept coming. I could see Booty crawling from the other side of the house with a box to hold the pups. The dog was now hot on the trail of the bone and Clyde said, "Now pull faster!"

I did, and soon the dog was at the edge of the house. I had backed up, but Clyde stayed right by the edge of the house. He waved to me to pull faster. I did, and the dog jumped into the sunlight. Clyde quickly grabbed her collar and the butt end of the tail at the same time.

"Let go of the rope, Tommy; she's got the bone," he yelled.

The dog was flailing away, and Clyde walked quickly to the dog run and threw her in. Slamming the gate he laughed, "Hell of a job! You boys did a hell of a good job. Booty, let's see those puppies."

Booty brought the box over, and Clyde said, "Well, I'll be damn. She didn't eat a one of the little monsters. All six are ok. You know what that means, Tommy?"

"No Sir. I don't."

"It means about $3,000. I can sell these puppies, and they'll bring a mighty fine coin. Catahoulas are scarce and fierce. You don't want them around children. These dogs are bred to hunt and kill especially wild hogs. You boys done real good. Real good.

"Now ya'll go wash up good. I'll take care of the puppies and their mama. She done good and deserves her hambone dog chow and plenty of water," said Clyde grinning as he picked up the box of puppies.

What a day. Booty got cleaned up outside with me. And then we made plans. "The next few days won't be much chores," Booty said. "I s'pect maybe we go blackberry pickin' in a few days."

"Sounds good to me. How far we got to go?" I asked.

Booty turned and pointed in the direction of Son's house and said, "Aunt Sue's got lots of blackberries and some a them be mighty ripe." He laughed.

I laughed too, at what I didn't know, but we were about to find a new adventure, and I was having the time of my young life. And soon I would find more excitement than I ever thought possible.

The week went by in a flash. Doing chores, visiting friends and other relatives kept me pretty busy. Then on a Saturday morning around 8:00am, I heard a soft knock on the house just below my window. "You ready to get some blackberries, Tommy?" Booty whispered loudly to me.

"Gimme 'bout 10 minutes," I said as I ran to quickly brush my teeth.

I got my jeans on and a clean t-shirt and started to the front door when I heard a booming voice say, "Where the hell you off to?"

I turned and Clyde stood there in his work pants and no shirt. "Booty and I are going to pick blackberries up yonder by Aunt Sue's," I said.

"That be so? Well, just keep your britches hiked up and belted tight. Don't want 'em droppin' down in that patch," he said.

"Yassuh," I said as I ran for the door, not having the faintest idea what he was talking about.

I ducked out the front door and left Clyde chuckling to himself; again about what, I didn't know. Booty was waiting at the bottom stair of the porch. He grinned and said, "Let's get to them berries."

We walked up the road toward Aunt Sue's house, and the closer we got, the more girls I saw coming out of the house. They were all carrying buckets or big white enamel bowls. They were laughing and having a grand old time. Some were pointing fingers at me and Booty and whispering; then they started laughing again.

We walked up and Booty said, "Dis my fren. He name be Tommy."

The girls all laughed and giggled and said, "Tommy, Tommy" over and over.

I didn't know much more to do than smile and say, "How ya'll doin'?"

Then they all laughed, and I swear I heard some whisper, "His skin be so white and pretty."

Booty just laughed with them then leaned into me and said, "Tommy, I think youse gonna get the pick of the litter."

"Who you goin' with Booty?" I asked.

Booty said, "Why, Tommy, I got me a special gal. You knows her, but you best get to pickin' cause times a flyin' by. I'll tell you all 'bout it when we gets them berries."

I stared at him for a moment then said, "Let's get started."

The girls all laughed, and off we went ambling through the bushes looking for berries. It wasn't long till a couple of girls my age were tagging along with me while hummin' a tune and pickin' berries. We were having a good time together or so it seemed to me. Finally, we came into a whole mess of blackberries.

The bushes were loaded, and it didn't take much work to get two buckets full. By this time, I was laughing with and at the girls, who were apparently flirting with me. They were pushing each other, one girl in particular, in my direction.

Looking at me somewhat shy, she said, "You be so pretty scept you not black, is you?"

I poetically replied, "No, I'm white as the clouds in the sky."

She said, "That be a nice way to say youse white, but I thinks you be best lookin' black."

And with that, she smeared blackberries all over my face. I was covered in blackberries and the girls were all laughing. Then one smeared another girl and suddenly we were all smashing and throwing blackberries. Laughing, the other girls walked off, while the one following me stayed behind.

We walked over to an old fence that was covered with blackberry bushes. I couldn't see the other kids, the road or Aunt Sue's house. We stood there a few minutes looking at each other for and then she said, "You want to look at me?"

"I am looking at you," I said, trying not to sound confused.

"No, I mean look at me with no clothes," she responded.

I choked for a minute then said, "I'm not sure 'bout what you're saying."

So, she lifted her gingham dress and was stark naked. "Now you show me what you be like," she said.

I stammered for a moment, but then she said, "Don't be 'fraid. Lookee, I ain't 'fraid."

And with that, she took her dress off and stood right in front of me. I looked around and didn't see anyone, so I started to take my shirt off. My pale white skin looked so fragile compared to the sleek, young girl, whose name I didn't know.

"Now show me everything," she said.

I started to undo my belt when we both heard Aunt Sue's crackling voice hollering, "Where you children be? Where's them berries you suppose be pickin'?"

The girl picked up her dress and slipped it over her head. Then she picked up a handful of blackberries and smeared them across my chest and stomach while saying,

"You come by tomorrow, and we'll pick more berries in my secret place."

Around a big oleander bush came Aunt Sue with her cane just a flyin'. "What you two are doing ovah heah? Mr. Tommy, how you don't get such a mess all ovah you? Sakes a live! What's Ms. Norma gonna do with you? And, girl, you get yourself cleaned up."

"Lord, have mercy; ya'll look like you been more playin' than pickin'. Now fill dese heah pails and get back to the house. I be cooking pies all night with the looks of both you."

She turned, cursing under her breath, and walked back to the old house. The girl looked straight at me and said, "Tommy be such a pretty name and you be such a pretty boy. You comin' back tomorrow?"

"I sure am, just soon as I get my chores done. I'll be here at 10am. And what are we going to do?" I replied.

"You be lucky if you see. I likes you, Tommy," she said.

I was scarlet red by this time and coated with blackberries. The thoughts running through my mind were like thoughts I never had before. A naked girl asking me to come back and see her. I was so excited I had a feeling like never before.

We both kept picking berries and slowly made our way to the house. Booty was waiting for me with a huge smile as he said, "I see you gots some berries, Tommy, but you supposed to have them in the pail, not all over yourself. Mr. Clyde is gonna have a good laugh and Ms. Norma's gonna be a stormin'. We best clean you up afore we walk to the Big House. Come with me."

We went to Aunt Sue's well, and Booty pulled up a bucket of water and poured it over me. Blackberry juice was flowing everywhere but I was coming clean. The young girl walked up with a worn towel. As I dried off, I asked her name.

She said, "That's for me to know and you to find out tomorrow. I be waitin'."

Booty grinned so big I thought he might break his jaw. "Ooh, Mr. Tommy, you going to get your tail twisted tomorrow. That gal be as sweet on you as bees on honey. But you be the king bee tomorrow. Yassuh, you be the king bee."

With that, I started putting on my shirt, and we walked toward the Big House. "Booty, what be that girls name?" I asked.

He looked at me and said, "Why, her name be Marcella, but we calls her Marcie. You best be careful with that gal. She's a hellcat if there ever was one. Ain't a feared of no one and knows what she wants. She be good friends with my gal, Nell."

"But my Nell ain't wild as Marcie. Nell, she gots a little boy name Robert. Ms. Robbye know her."

"Marcie?" I said. "I kinda like that name. I guess I'll see her tomorrow."

"Now you best be careful with that Marcie. She has ways about her. She likes to tease boys. So maybe she sees you; maybe she don't. But if I was you, I be trying to find some berries with that gal."

"Booty, you say you're kinda sweet on that gal name of Nell? I think I know that gal. I saw her when I was staying at my aunt Robbye's last year in Jackson Landing."

"Yassuh, she be the one. She sweet, smart and lucky to be alive. You knew about the big wreck?" Booty said.

"Oh yeah, and that crazy Watson," I replied.

With that, Booty got real quiet. Then he finally said, "He was a bad man, Tommy. Real bad and crazy drunk most time. She got bad hurt in that wreck with that crazy drunk nigger. I knew him from the time I was stayin' at Mam's out in Mr. DeLee's woods."

"Most of us stayed clear of that Watson but he bought my Nell from Mam. I saw him give her the money but my Nell ain't have no say. One day she was just gone."

I said, "Booty, I didn't know you was raised at Mam's. I was out there many times with Aunt Robbye helping with the groceries and such that she got from the government food program. And all that candy. Why I must have seen you but never met you."

"And I knew Watson too. Yeah I seen him up real close. To damn close. He liked to scared the hell out of me and my brother. I'll be damn, Booty, now you and Nell together. Ain't life somethin'? Booty, I think I know why you and I are becoming good friends."

He looked shocked and said, "What you be tryin' to say, Tommy?"

"Just that you're a person who cares about other folk. You've got a good heart, and a forgiving soul. I feel good around that kinda person."

I wondered if anyone other than the folk in my family had ever said something kind to him.

Booty puffed up with pride and asked, "Even though I be black…and you be white?" He said, sounding confused.

"Why, hell yeah. But I didn't know youse black?" I said with a playful grin.

With that, I gave him a friendly shove and he said, "Blackberry pickin'. You don picked the right gal for the wrong reasons."

"But," he said with a big grin, "you gonna have a real show. Blackberry pickin'," he laughed and laughed.

As we walked up to the Big House, Norma was standing on the porch with a mighty strong stare looking like it was aimed at me. I guess I did look pretty durned foolish. Clothes all messed and me with blackberries still in my hair and ears; hell, I looked like a ragged mess.

Norma stood still with arms folded and said, "Where them berries? I'm supposed to be making blackberry cobbler for the Greenwood Ladies Club. And I don't see enough berries to make a thing, much less a cobbler. So, what you gonna do about it, Mr. Smarty Pants Tommy?"

"I guess I'll go first thing tomorrow morning and pick some more," I sheepishly replied.

With that, Booty laughed so hard that he could hardly breathe. Norma huffed, turned and walked into the house and hollered, "Clyde, your blood kin be following in your footsteps."

Clyde yelled, "I can't hear a durn word you're saying; something 'bout stepping on feet?"

Norma laughingly said, "Tommy says he hurt his foot and needs more berry picking time for my cobbler."

"Well, tell him to go get more but not tomorrow. In fact, it may be good for him to not go runnin' around for a few days. I think it best that he and Booty go over to Jackson Landing for a while."

"Things are about to get a bit rough around here. I'm afraid we may get some visitors who'd just as soon see me gone as see me at all," yelled Clyde.

I walked back to Clyde and Norma's room and knocked on the door. "C'mon in, I know it's you, Tommy," said Clyde.

I opened the door slowly and walked in to find Clyde sitting in a rocking chair, cleaning and oiling his 12-gauge Browning semi-automatic shotgun with an over and under 20 gauge lying on the bed. "What's on your mind," Clyde said, not looking up from working on the gun.

"Well, Uncle Clyde, I was hoping to go back and get them berries tomorrow since it's too late to go back today. But you think it's best if I go back to Aunt Robbye's tomorrow?"

"Well," Clyde said without looking away from the gun, "some serious folk from Northwood are a telling me that some of those relatives of that young son-of-a bitch who got smart at the ballgame might be paying us a visit. I ain't sure when and if they might show up. Booty can't help cause he's the one they're really after."

"Your aunt Norma is up front now telling him where he needs to be heading and to stay out of sight for a few days till this thing either blows over or blows up. Your aunt Robbye is on her way over with your brother and Ruth's .38 pistol. Uncle Son and his boys will be around. They'll have a couple shotguns, too."

"We'll be loadin' the guns with buckshot and rock salt. If they show and try to bring on some shenanigans, we'll blow them down. So, I s'pect this might just blow over but gotta be ready if it blows up. How's that sound to you?"

"More exciting than going to Robbye's or pickin' blackberries with them young gals running around with no underwear up at Aunt Sue's?"

I was pretty durn near scared to death. It sounded to me like the fun I was a planning might be more like a war fixing to start.

"Now you ain't pullin' my leg, Uncle Clyde…are you?" I asked.

Clyde looked up from the gun and said, "Boy, I don't fool around with jokes about the Klan. I hate them, and they hate me. But by God, they want a fight, then they'll face the wrath of the Fitzhughs should they try something stupid."

I had never heard Clyde talk so direct and determined. He stared at me hard with a blaze in his eyes, lighting a fire in me that would burn in me for the rest of my life. Clyde determinedly said, "You always stay true to your values no matter what the stakes. Stay true to family. That's what I was taught, and that's what you best learn."

Norma came walking to the back of the house and said, "Sister's here with Will. They got the .38 and a .22 rifle. Son called and said he and son, James, just home from the army, would be ready in half an hour. Eva was frying chicken. They'll be bringing that, some cornbread and 'plenty of fire power', as Son said."

Clyde simply nodded his head. Norma reached into her closet and pulled a big colt .44 from the top shelf. She began loading it and put some more shells in the pocket of her kitchen apron. Clyde loaded the 12 gauge, picked up Norma's 20 gauge, stood up and said, "Let's go see Sister."

Aunt Robbye and Will were waiting on the front porch. I was surprised that Norma hadn't invited them in, but I figured that she didn't want Robbye or Will to see the arsenal that Clyde was creating. But then Clyde quickly pushed the screen door open and walked out carrying the big semi-automatic 12 gauge.

He gave Norma the other shotgun and she had a big .44 in a holster that I'd not seen. Robbye gave nervous look and asked, as she pointed to the shotguns, "Clyde, is this going to get that serious?"

He looked downright mean and angry as he said, "Them Franklin boys from Northwood said they were hungry for a fight. I don't want it, but I figure I best be ready. Robbye you take Tommy and Will back to Jackson Landing. You can squeeze Mr. Booty here into your car. He's the one that caused all of this."

Booty hung his head in dismay when Clyde reached out and pulled him to his side and gave him a big hug and said, "You know I'm just picking on you right?"

Booty looked up at Clyde and said, "Mr. Clyde, I'd never do anything to hurt you and if you want I'll stay and do whatever you wants me to do."

Clyde actually kissed him on the forehead and said, "I know, I know. Now you all get a going. Norma will call when and if we need help. So be ready. And Tommy lay off the booze."

Robbye looking startled said, "Clyde, you haven't let that boy be drinking, have you?"

Clyde roared with laughter and Norma knowingly grinned as Clyde said, "I gotcha didn't I, sister? Now get in the car and call when your home. I'll hold down the fort. Don't worry. Those Northwood boys will call ahead of time. They're all a bunch of show off sons a bitches."

He looked at me and Will and said, "You boys be ready if we need you?"

"Yessir," Will replied. "We'll be ready to help any way we can."

Clyde said, "Good, I'll take your word on that. Now get going. And Booty lay low."

As we all piled into Aunt Robbye's car, we saw Uncle Son walking toward the Big house with his oldest son, James.

"Well, good. Here comes Son and James. Looks like they're loaded for a war," said Clyde.

Aunt Robbye started the car, waved to Son and James and hollered, "Call when we're needed."

Son reached out and opened the gate. He and James walked up to the porch. "Well, has the fightin' started or have you already whooped their ass?" Son said.

"Nope, we're just waiting to see if they'll make an appearance. Come up in the house and take a load off. You got some chicken with you? I s'pect everyone might be hungry," Clyde said.

"Bring it on back to the kitchen, and we'll wait on the back porch till any action starts. James, you remember how to shoot that damn thing?"

James replied, "They mess with us, they got a fight comin'. We'll knock 'em down; that's for damn sure. Will someone pass me a Coke? Any Grandad to chase it?"

"Nope, not till the fighting's done. Son, the chicken any good?" Clyde said.

"Yassuh, right off the stove. Eva spiced it real good. Got some straight up Coke Colas if anyone wants one," Son said as he set the fried chicken on the kitchen table.

Everyone dug in and ate, knowing if the fight came it would pull the energy level to high gear. This was gonna be a true show down. Clyde looked at James as they all reached for the bag of food and asked, "James, you have this much fun in the army?"

James laughed and said, "Well, sorta. I was over in a place called Viet-Nam trying to teach them boys how to fight. But this little scuffle looks like we could see some real sparks."

With that answer, James passed out Cokes to anyone who wanted one.

Norma said she had sweet iced tea if anyone cared to have a glass. No one replied. It was obvious all nerves were running pretty hot.

The day passed slowly and tension filled the eerily still Louisiana evening. Not a leaf moving as the sun slipped slowly beyond the Spanish moss-covered oak trees behind the Big House. The hounds were fed, yet unsettled with the smell of the guns and shells that lined the side of the front porch.

Clyde said to James, "You take the first watch. When you get tired, get me or your pa and we'll give you a break. These Northwood yahoos usually get pretty lit up and bragging then give a call before they start their move. So we should have plenty of time."

"I s'pect it might just be around 3 or 4am. So just be on watch and prepared. Got it?"

James replied, "Yassuh, we'll be ready."

Son and Clyde retired to the back porch with a pot of coffee. Soon both were sound asleep. Waiting was in their hunting blood and they both new rest was gonna come in handy soon enough. Norma laid down in the bedroom with her latest crime novel and .44 by her side. Slowly, she closed her eyes and slept soundly to the noise of the two men snoring on the back porch.

James was the first to hear the telephone ringing. It was 5 AM and Eva, James mother, had just come on duty at the switchboard. She nervously said, "James, wake up your pa and Clyde. Them Northwood boys called and said they were coming for supper. And you know what that means."

"Yes, I do. Now call Ms. Robbye and let her know to get the boys and the guns and ammunition and get over here sooner the better." James walked to the back porch where his pa and Clyde were drinking coffee that Norma had just made.

She brought a cup to James and said, "Food will be out in a few. Are we all ready?"

Clyde looked at Son and said, "Yep, damn talky thing woke us up from a nice restful sleep. We're ready. James, are Robbye and the boys on their way?"

"Yes sir, Mama is calling them now. They should be here in about 30 or 40 minutes."

"Good," Son said, "we're gonna need 'em all."

Finally Robbye showed up. Her 56 Ford turned the corner into Greenwood and she blew the horn as she drove by the telephone terminal building. Eva waved out the window then sat back in her chair and prayed. She knew a fight was a comin'.

Everyone at the big house gathered on the front porch as the Ford pulled up to the front of the house. Will and Tommy got our carrying a .22 long semi-automatic that held 17 long rifle shots and Ruth's .38 long barreled pistol. Clyde hollered at Robbye and said, "Drive around to the back of the big house and park the car. Don't want it all shot to pieces."

After everyone had gathered on the front porch, Clyde gave the instructions. "Son, you and James stand behind the big oak trees on either side of the house. Take your shot guns and plenty of ammunition."

"Son, you get buckshot and, James, you take deer slugs if needed. If they fire first, then fire back and don't stop until they give up or can't move. Will you get under the house with that .22 and shoot the tires out on the truck or car whatever they and anyone else are driving."

"Norma, you blow away the front end of the car or truck. Shoot for the radiator and engine. Then aim for the windshield."

Norma asked, "Clyde, where will you be?"

I'll stand here on the front porch with my Browning and blow 'em from the side as fast as I can shoot. But all of y'all let them shoot first. Then blow them down. If they're aiming for a fight, they'll shoot at me first.

"If I see a gun come up, I'll move behind the column next to the step. That's the sign for all of you to blast the hell out of them. We all know what to do?"

Robbye asked, "What about me. Clyde?"

"You stay inside but keep Ruth's .38 close. If any of them get out of the car, shoot 'em. Then call the sheriff. Are we all set to have some wild ass fun?" Everyone nodded yes.

Clyde said. "Now we wait."

The afternoon passed slowly with the tension growing. Will these Klan rednecks really show up?

The answer came around 4pm.

Everyone kept a sharp look out in the distance at the turnoff into the town. Then the phone rang; it was Ms. Minnie.

Norma answered and then turned to the screen front door, and yelled, "It's them. They're in a red pick-up and an old black 4 door sedan. Looks like 2 men in the truck cab, 2 in the back. And 4 men in the sedan. I see some rifles or shotguns. They're headed our way."

Norma said, "Thanks, Minnie, we've got them in our sights. Robbye will call if we need help from the sheriff."

Minnie stammered, "Lord Lord, Norma, y'all take care and knock those no counts down, they's scum."

Clyde told Son, "Go to the left side of the porch and, James, go to the right. Be sure and stand behind those big oaks and remember don't fire unless they shoot first. If they do, let 'em have it. Norma, you stand here next to me. I want them to see that hogs leg pistol of yours. Will, Tommy, get under the porch like I told you."

"Remember if the shooting starts, Will, aim that .22 at their tires. If they fire first, start shooting. I don't want them leaving until we're finished with them. Robbye, go in the house and take that .38. If things get bad for us, call Sheriff Ben, and tell him to hurry."

Then he ordered everyone saying, "All right, no shooting till they shoot. Everyone answer if you understand. If there's any real damage done, this has got to be self-defense."

Each of us hollered 'ready'. It wasn't until that point that I realized how damn dangerous this put down really was. Clyde was tough. But the thought of him killing someone or him being killed had never crossed my mind. Yet here we all were, watching the truck and car slowly make the final turn and head down the road to the Big House.

The truck slowed as they came closer and stopped in front of the house. A big-bellied man with a ball cap on that said 'Northwood' got out and sauntered over to the fence. He looked slowly from one end of the porch to the other then focused on Clyde and Norma.

"Whewee! Looks like you got a goddamn army here, Clyde. Plan to use it?" He yelled across the yard.

"Depends on you and your bunch, Johnnie. You be the one doing the talkin', so I hear. That be right?" Clyde responded.

"Yep, that be right. You was talkin' pretty tough to my brother at that ballgame a few weeks past, and what you said kinda pissed me off. The way I sees it, a nigger is a nigger. And just where is that nigger boy you been keeping?" Johnnie asked.

"Well, you sees it however you want to, but no one talks to my boys that way, especially at a ballgame where I'm umpire. Now you've said your piece, so I s'pect you need to get back in that truck and head north," said Clyde with conviction.

"That ain't gonna happen unless you either bring that nigger out here for a whoopin' or we come get him," said Johnnie.

Clyde lowered the shotgun and aimed directly at Johnnie. "Now here's what's gonna happen. You're gonna turn around, get your fat ass in the truck, drive out of my town, and keep going until you're safe at home with a nice cup of coffee. Am I right?"

With that, Johnnie tipped his hat toward Norma and said, "Good evening, ma'am." He turned and walked to the other side of the truck. Then the first shot was fired and hit Clyde in the left shoulder. Clyde's shotgun fired blowing out the window of the pick-up truck. Then all hell broke loose.

Son and James had the truck and the car in a crossfire, and they didn't aim high. The trucks windshield shattered, and the car windows were blown out. Then, Will let loose with the .22 and shot out the tires on the truck and a front tire on the car.

Clyde let loose with two more blasts directly at the truck. Aunt Norma was firing her .44 pistol at the car as fast as she could pull the trigger. And then the gunfire stopped almost as soon as it had started.

I saw Johnnie's hat waving above the hood of the truck. He was yelling, "Stop the shooting. Enough been hurt already."

Clyde's shoulder was bleeding. Apparently, not life threatening, but Norma was already putting a large bandage and wrapping it tightly with a clean dish cloth from the kitchen. Clyde stood and spoke in a loud determined voice and said, "Johnnie, get your damn truck moved away from my house. Anybody killed?"

"No but my brother, Frank, and two others got a big load of buckshot and glass. I think the boys in the car got banged up pretty bad and scared the hell out of 'em," Johnnie replied.

"Too bad. You keep hangin' around here for another minute, and we'll blast you all to hell. You hear? Now get in your truck and move on down the road. I'm tired of talkin' and tired of hearin' you whine."

"So, move, and don't you dare show your goddamn face in Greenwood again or I'll have to kill you, Johnnie, and your dumb ass brother," Clyde shouted as he quickly re-loaded his shotgun.

"But, Clyde, my brother's hurt pretty bad," pleaded Johnnie. "Can't you at least get us to a doctor or the clinic. We need some help."

"Well, so do I, Johnnie, but you brought this on yourself. Your brother fired the first shot, and he meant to kill me. But he's such a dumb shit, he missed. So, we blew your ass down, and like I said, we will do it again if you bring your sorry bunch of redneck Klan south of Northwood."

"Now get out of that truck and get your idiot brother in the car and get to your own doctor. You can fix your tire up by the Esso station. Go on before we open up on you again," Clyde threatened and stood his ground as Norma kept working on the bandages trying to stop the bleeding.

With that said, Johnnie got Frank out of the truck, and they limped back toward the car. Both were pretty shot up with buckshot and rock salt from somebody's gun. They slowly drove out of town with one flat tire on the car and turned into the Esso station on the highway.

I got out from under the house and carefully walked out to the truck and opened the doors. It looked like someone got hit pretty good. Blood was all over the front seat. Clyde looked at me and said, "Tommy, get some rags, wipe the seat clean of glass and blood, and let's see if she'll start up."

After a good wipe down, I jumped in, found the keys in the ignition and sure enough the old truck started on the first try. "Now turn her around and drive it down to the old Stanley house," Clyde instructed.

"The tires are flat," I stammered.

"I know the damn tires are flat," he said harshly. "But make it work. We ain't gonna welcome the sheriff with a bloody shot-up truck. Now get it going," Clyde said as he winced in pain from his shoulder wound.

Son and James came over and helped me get the damn truck to move, flat tire and all. The interior smelled like blood and whiskey, and I kept gagging from the odor. But, did as told. The old truck barely made the end of the road to my aunt Ruth's old, abandoned house.

I parked in the field next to the house. As I stopped, I watched as Clyde pulled up in the Bird and slowly got out with a big can of gas. He groaned in pain as he poured the gasoline in and around the truck. He angrily threw the empty tank into the truck and told me to stand back.

Then he lit the truck on fire. Turned to me and said calmly, "Let's go, Tommy; you drive. I'm worn to the bone."

I got in the car, as Clyde handed me a bottle of old Grandad bourbon, and said, "Have a drink; it'll calm your nerves. I hope you've learned that you really gotta show redneck scum you mean business. And remember don't ever let up until the other son-of-a-bitch can't stand up. Fight 'em as hard as you can."

"Never forget that, boy. The last man standing is the winner in a fight. And you just saw a hell of a good one. Mighty proud of you and Will."

I took a long drink of the Old Grandad, which scalded my throat but actually tasted pretty damn good. It did calm me but also made me a little woozy. I managed to drive and asked Clyde, "How's the shoulder?"

Clyde slowly but determinedly replied, "I've got a few more fights left in me. I'll make it."

We were back at the Big House when we heard a big explosion. I turned and looked out the car window at a big fireball. The truck was a blur of flames; quite an event for a little town. But no one came out to see the commotion, nor did I ever hear anyone talk about the fire.

The sheriff never showed up or asked Clyde any questions. The sheriff knew the story and knew the answers. He knew the Fitzhughs were serious and honorable folk. No questions asked. No answers needed.

We got out of the car and walked to the gate. Clyde stumbled but said he was ok. He collapsed in his well-worn metal yard chair. "Guess I'm more tired than I thought. Please ask Norma to get me a big glass of sweet tea and a half of glass of my hidey-hole Granddad?" Clyde asked.

I went to the back of the house and Norma was sitting there holding her .44 colt. She looked at me and asked, "Is it done?"

"Yes. I don't think that bunch will ever show themselves south of Northwood. They met their match. Where's Son and James?" I asked.

"They're cleaning up out back. They want to make sure Clyde's ok and that those Northwood bastards keep heading north," she replied.

Son and James checked on Clyde and told Norma they needed to get him to a doctor as soon as possible. Son said he was thirsty, so we wouldn't be seeing him for a day or two; when Son went on a drinking binge, you wouldn't go near him until every drop of alcohol in the house was gone.

Eva would take the keys to their truck and move in with her sister in the Landing until he finally sobered up. James said he would drive to Angola and get a doctor who they knew was on good terms with the Fitzhughs and would patch Clyde up. Nothing was to be said about the shootout. James got in his new Ford and sped off toward Angola.

I walked back into the kitchen and told Norma, "Clyde said he wants a big glass of sweet tea and half a glass of Grandad."

"Tell him to hang on; it's on its way. He took a hell of a shot, Tommy. Don't let him go to sleep; keep the bandage secure around that hole in his shoulder," she quickly replied.

I ran down the hallway and pushed the screen door open and looked for Clyde. He was sitting in the yard staring through the fence out to the baseball field.

"Are you ok?" I said.

"Oh yeah, just a little tired. Kinda rough and tumble a while ago. Don't ya think?" Clyde said.

I nervously laughed and said, "Well, lemme just say I damn near crapped my britches. But luckily, I didn't."

Clyde laughed just as Norma came out with the tea and a healthy shot of bourbon. "Give the boy the whiskey. He needs another drop to soothe his nerves. I'll take a slug, and then I'll take the tea. I'm parched and feeling a little dizzy," said Clyde.

"James has gone to Angola to get the doc. You're gonna need some sewing up. Good thing the bullet went straight through without hitting any bone. Let's get you inside to lie down. I'm gonna clean your wound and re-do the bandages. You need to rest," instructed Norma.

"Alright," agreed Clyde as he got to his feet. "Anyone else get some lead?"

"No one but you and the side of our house. I unloaded my .44 on the back-up car. Blew out the head lights so, I must have put a shot in the engine, or at least the radiator, but I didn't set the damn thing on fire like you, Mister barn-burner man," said Norma.

With that, she laughed and gave Clyde a hug, carefully avoiding his bandaged left shoulder. "You s'pect they'll be back?" She asked.

"Nope. I don't think them boys will do much of anything, much less try and tussle with the Fitzhughs again," Clyde said confidently.

With that reassurance, I took a scalding sip of the bourbon and handed the glass to Clyde. He swallowed the remaining Grandad. Robbye came out the door and said, "Will, you and Tom get your things together, we need to get home soon. Your grandmother will be worried sick."

Will spoke up quickly saying, "Aunt Robbye, call her and tell her we're fine. I think we should stay here tonight. Things seem a little tight right now, and this may not be the end of the trouble."

Robbye looked surprised. Her nephews had become men in a matter of weeks. Not just men but men who would stand up for their family no matter the odds. Her surprise quickly turned to pride.

Whatever Clyde's shortcomings, he could pull the best out of most people. He had put his young nephews to the test, and they had proven they were family blood.

"Why sure you can stay tonight. I'll be back early tomorrow," said Robbye.

Looking at Norma, she reached out and both women hugged each other. Then, staring at each other for a moment, they hugged again. They both felt it; this was family.

"Sister," Clyde called. "Tell everyone we're all fine. James went for the doctor. Call later after you get to the house. Take Ruth's .38. I know she feels naked without it."

Everyone laughed. Clyde just couldn't help himself. After going out back where her car was parked, she got in and cranked up the Ford. Then, waving goodbye, she headed back to Jackson Landing.

I was sure she had a couple of strong drinks when she got home. She was pretty shaken up. But then, who wasn't?

Will was given a room to sleep in; the one next to mine. We were all tired and were in bed by 8pm. I drifted off into a deep slumber. I guess it was around 10pm when I heard someone whispering. I looked up from my pillow and came almost face to face with Will.

"What are you doing?" I asked through a sleepy fog.

"There's somebody outside smoking a Bull Durham cigarette. I can smell it. Can't you smell it?" Will said.

By this time, I was wide awake, so I got up and went to the window. I looked out and shone a flashlight. Flashlights were quite handy on nights when you had to pee.

I saw nor smelled anything. "Will, go back to bed. We have a big day with lots of work. So, go get some sleep. There's nothing outside."

He argued but finally went back to his room, and I fell into a deep sleep. Will and I left the next morning as soon as we had coffee and something to eat. I drove him back to the French House. When he got out of the car, he said, "You be careful over there. That little town is like a bomb ready to go off."

I didn't stop to speak to anyone. I was anxious to get back to Greenwood and see how everyone was doing. Will never spent the night in Greenwood again.

I drove back to Greenwood rolling along at a pretty good clip. Took the Bird up to about 75 just to say I'd done it. When I got to Greenwood, I saw Booty sitting on the front porch of the Big House, apparently waiting to hear my side of the showdown.

"Tommy, How you be doin'? Boy, I hear there be some real shoot-em-up going on whilst I been laying low," said Booty.

"Yeah, it got pretty damn wild. Did you know Ms. Norma had that big ol .44?" I said.

"Why sure I did. She musta showed me that big ol thing five or six times. One tough woman to handle a big ol gun like that one be. 'Lordy, Lordy who done shot Shorty.' That be what she likes to say when she finish shooting," Booty said smiling.

"I see her a shootin'. It was somethin' like I never saw before and hope I don't never see again. Liked to scared me good when she lifted that big ol pistol and started firing. I don't think she killed anyone, but she damn sure hit one of them trash bastards."

"There was blood all over the ground. Son shot the hell out of the car in the front I mean, it was like a war. We really whipped their butts," I said.

"I hear that Mr. Clyde got shot? He be alright, though?" Booty asked concerned.

"Yeah, got hit in the shoulder but didn't hit no bone. Bullet went plum through. But he's in a bit of pain. He's resting right now. Doctor patched him up real good."

"Doc did a lot of stitching and gave him a bunch of pills to help him heal, but I know he'll need a warm bath to clean up. He had blood all over him," I replied.

We went on talking about the gun battle, the girls up the street and how Clyde was going to handle the potential revenge from the Klan, all this while feeding the hounds.

Booty mowed the lawn and drew water from the well for Norma, who started heating it on the stove. She asked me to wake Clyde and tell him his bathwater was about ready.

Clyde got out of the bed slowly and said, "Guess I best clean up and check this shoulder."

With that, he stripped down, got into the tub and sat all hunched up waiting for the hot water. "How'd the Bird act while you drove Will home? Did you notice the wobble in the left front tire after it hit 60?" Clyde asked.

"You know it did start to wobble around 70," I replied.

Clyde roared with laughter saying, "Gotcha again. I told you not to take the Bird over 60, didn't I?"

Stammering, I replied, "Yep, you sure did, but I wanted to make sure that she was running good enough to outrun anyone that might be chasing us."

Just then, Norma walked in as Clyde was laughing at his 'Gotcha Joke'. "You ready for some warm water? Or do you want to just sit there naked as a laughing jay bird?" She asked.

"Well, pour me some water, and I'll get started. But Tommy here needs to get out and help Booty. Tommy's stories are gonna give me a hernia from laughing," Clyde said.

I headed outside and told Booty that Clyde was doing fine. So, we finished up our chores and watched as Norma heated more water for Clyde's bath. She worked on his shoulder, putting more iodine on it and re-wrapping the bandage.

Norma thought he was enjoying his soak a little too long, so she hollered, "Clyde, what the Sam Hill are you doing in there?"

"I'm working on my differential," he yelled back.

"What's he talking 'bout?" I asked Norma.

"He's working on his rear end, doctoring his hemorrhoids," she said. Enough information for me.

"Where's Booty?" Norma asked.

"I think he's gone up the street to see Nell. Want me to go get him?" I said anxiously.

"No. Let him cut up a little. There will be plenty of work to do fixing the windows and digging out the bullets in the front of the house. What do you say we go over to Angola and get some Chinese takeout? Clyde's got a hankering for something different; besides, he needs his rest, and we'll be back in an hour," said Norma.

"Sounds good to me," I said. "Can I drive?"

"You got your license yet?" Norma asked.

"No, ma'am. I ain't old enough," I replied.

"Well, no matter. Ain't no one gonna stop us," she said as she went to check on Clyde. "Clyde, we're going to get some food you want anything special?"

"Just something Chinese, whatever you and the boy want. But don't let him go over 60 in the Bird."

She chuckled saying, "Whatever you say. Now get some rest. That shoulder could get worse."

We walked to the car. I saw Booty walking down the road holding hands with Nell who was holding little Robert. They waved as I put the car in first gear; then Norma and I sped off to Angola.

We drove a while before either of us spoke. Not wanting to break Clyde's trust in me, I kept the Bird at a steady 55 mph. Finally, Norma said, "We've had some busy times; you 'bout tired of all this redneck excitement?"

"Why, no, ma'am. I'm having a great time. I haven't had this much fun ever in life," I said, and meant every word of it.

She harrumphed and said, "You know your uncle Clyde has a bad heart?" I looked at her for what seemed a moment and almost ran off the road.

"Yes, I know, but it ain't bad, is it?" I finally said.

"Tommy, it's been bad since he was a young man. That's what kept him out of the wars. His heart is weak and don't beat right. I'm worried about him. In fact, I'm surprised he ain't dead yet," she said as she gazed out the window.

I looked at her again, and then stared at the road as I drove, too shocked to speak. "You mean he really could die?" I finally said.

"Afraid so. I've been with him so long and been through so much with his drinking and roustabout ways that I thought he was never gonna be gone. But now, I'm worried. He needs to rest. Take the stress off his life. I think the Klan boys learned their lesson, and they won't be bothering us no more. But I do think you need to go back to Robbye's and let him settle down."

"Booty can handle things, and you've grown a lot just in the last few weeks. Clyde will come see you at Robbye's. Besides, you need to go back to school soon, and I'm sure your mom and dad miss you, and Will. So, I'll talk to Clyde tonight and plan on taking you to the French House tomorrow. Is that ok with you?" Norma said.

I was so surprised that I could hardly speak and drive. So, I just said, "Yes."

"Good. Now let's get some food and get back to the Big House. Clyde will be waiting, but we won't say a thing to him about you leaving tomorrow. I'll tell him when the times right. Now this don't mean you won't be seeing us. We love you, Tommy."

"You've become the closest thing to a true friend that Booty ever had. And you're white. That ain't the way it works in the South. Don't you ever forget that. But we're different. We respect people for what they do in life, not just who they are or their color."

"That's just the way we are, and so are you and your brother and mom and dad. Family is just life showing itself. Never forget that, Tommy," she said.

We got the Chinese food and went home. Clyde was in a good mood. Dinner was nice, and neither Norma nor I said anything, until after we finished eating.

Finally, Norma said, "Tommy, there's a baseball game at the Angola mental health facility tomorrow. You want to go? Clyde, are you still going to try and go to work tomorrow?"

"Yes, ma'am. I called Woodie Summerton, just like you asked me to, and he said to come in tomorrow and help with scheduling road projects. Hell, I don't know nothing about scheduling, but he said to come on in and he'd put me on the parish payroll for a while. Guess the word about the gunfire got some folk's attention."

"So, Tommy, go on with your aunt Norma, and we'll visit tomorrow after my new job," Clyde said as he ate his chicken chowmein.

"Look forward to it, Uncle Clyde. Just sorry I can't drive you," I said.

"Why sure you can drive. Those ballgames with the crazies don't start till mid-day. Right, Norma?" Clyde said.

"Yes, that's right. Tommy, you drive your uncle to work, and I'll pick him up later. Now who's eating the rest of that chop suey?" She asked.

They both looked at me, and I grabbed the last spoon full and wolfed it down.

I tried to remember what I had seen and what I would miss. My mind was heavy with the thought that all the excitement, friendship and lessons I learned from Clyde, and how it was coming to an end. That night we all went to bed early. I laid awake thinking and suddenly broke into tears.

Where was all of this, and life itself, taking me? Difficult thoughts for me. My heart actually ached. It'd seemed as if my big adventure would go on forever. But reality snuck in the door and slammed the dream shut. It was about to end.

At 6am, Clyde stood at my door and said, "Sleeping's over. Time to get to work. Clean up and get dressed. I can't drive to work with this bum shoulder."

I dressed, walked out to the front porch and there he was grinning from ear to ear. "Let's see if that Yellow Bird will fly."

We got in, and I started the car. We took off for the highway barn. As we got up on the highway, Clyde said, "Put the pedal to the metal until I say slow down. Got it?"

"Got it," I said pushing the gas pedal to the floor.

The little Buick took off like a rocket. We were doing 60 in nothing flat. Clyde looked straight ahead and said, "Stay on it."

I did. Then we hit 80, and I thought for sure he'd say slow down. But he looked straight ahead and said, "Push it."

And then we hit 100, and he finally said, "You ever been a hundred miles an hour in your life?"

"Nope," I responded, wondering what he would say next.

"Slow her down. You've been there now. Plus, you've been in some serious fights. You've discovered girls. You gotta a life-long friend in Booty. You saw a man shot. You've seen how mean and terrible men can be to each other, simply because of the color of their skin."

"Hell, you had to watch Son shave. You used an outhouse and drank water from a well. You're fast becoming a grown man, and what's more, I love you like a son. Now slow the damn Bird down; we're almost at work," Clyde said softly.

I looked at him and for the first time ever I saw tears from his eyes rolling down his tanned cheeks. We pulled into the parking lot and both sat in the car. Clyde said, "I know you'll be leaving this afternoon, but that don't mean I won't be seeing you. I'll be over in a day or two, and we'll raise a little hell."

"Now get back to the Big House. Norma will be anxious. And remember keep the Bird under 60." He leaned over and gave me a big hug and said, "I really will miss you, and I love you with all my old heart."

He got out the door, waved and walked into the job trailer. I turned the Bird around got up on the highway and headed back to Greenwood for what I thought would be the last time. I cruised along at 60, doing fine, but then started to cry.

My summer—going from a boy to a would-be man, was coming to an end. An end I didn't ever want to see.

I pulled into the dirt parking area across from the house, and there was Robbye's old Ford waiting to take me back to my old life. She bounded down the stairs alone carrying a couple of paper bags filled with my clothes. She said, "Get in, and let's go. I don't want no more trouble and Greenwood is full of nothing but."

Holding back my tears I said, "But I was supposed to go to a ballgame with Norma."

"Another day; now get in the car," Robbye said with a look that told me not to argue with her.

I got in the car and off we went. Not a word was said between us until we reached the French House.

Robbye opened her door to get out and said, "Now nobody here knows what went on with you and Will and those son-a-bitches from Northwood the other day, so don't be talking about it to no one. You promise?"

I looked straight at her and said, "Not a word from me. I promise."

"Alright," she said. "Let's go see about some coffee and a little eye opener."

The day went on fine. Will and I walked down to the big pond hoping to not run across any water moccasins. We were both scared to death of snakes. Didn't see any while we talked quietly about the wild adventure we had gone through.

Will was still pretty shaken up. Me? I thought it was pretty damn fun, but then I was always a bit on the hell-raising, razor-walking side of life.

Will said, "Did you hear if any of those men got killed?"

"Naw, but I know the one that yelled at me and Booty at the ballgame got a load of buck and salt shot," I replied.

Surprisingly, Will said, "Serves the white trash right. He should know now to never pick a fight with a Fitzhugh."

"Damn straight," I replied. Then asked, "Say how'd your date with that girl from the malt shop work out?"

"Pretty good. These country girls get frisky after a couple of beers," Will answered.

I was surprised and asked, "Where the hell did you get the beer? You never told me about that."

Will looked at me and said, "Faucheaux's where else. I just told Luke I was 18 and he sold me a six pack of JAX."

"Damn," I replied. "I've got to give that a try." We both laughed as I said, "Well, this has been a hell of a summer. When are you leaving to see Mom and Dad?"

Will replied, "Robbye's taking me to the airport early tomorrow morning. I'll get to California by tomorrow night."

Startled, I replied, "I didn't know you were leaving so soon."

Will said, "College bound. Gotta get in school. Old man time is catching up with us both."

"Yep, I think I aged ten years after the shootout at Clyde and Norma's. I'm gonna miss you, big brother." With that, we hugged each other walked back to the house and drank a couple of Will's beers. What a time we'd had.

That evening, I went to bed early. The ceiling fans kept the house cool, and I slept like there was no tomorrow. Except there was.

Ruth came to the door of my room early the next morning and said, "You got company. Coffee's on the stove. Stay out of the brandy."

Startled, I hopped out of bed, cleaned up a bit and walked into the kitchen. Clyde was drinking coffee and talking to Ruth. Will and Robbye had already gone to the airport.

Clyde looked at me and said, "Morning! Come on out back. I brought you a little something to keep you busy while you're stuck here with the women folk."

He chuckled as Ruth said, "Go on, Tommy, see what Clyde's brought you."

Clyde pushed the screen door open, and we walked into the back yard. Tied to a 4x4 holding up the clothesline was a rail thin English Pointer. He stood up as Clyde and I walked toward him. The dog's ribs poked from either side.

He stood still, except for a tremble that seemed close to a complete shake. The dog was really scared. As we walked up, Clyde put his hand forward, knuckles first, to let the dog know he wasn't a threat.

"He's yours, Tommy, if you choose to keep him. Found him on the way over here. Somebody dumped him, and from the looks of him, he ain't been eatin' much and is loaded with ticks and fleas. Want him?"

Without hesitation, I said, "Yeah, I would love to have him. Can you help me work with him?"

Clyde hesitated, but then said, "Sure, if you want. I'll be glad to help. But my bum shoulder won't let me do much lifting and for sure no shooting. He's pretty gun shy. You'll have to work on that after you get him cleaned up and fed. You ready to start?"

"Yessir, I'm ready right now. I'm gonna name him Pete," I said grinning from ear to ear.

"Good name," said Clyde. "I've got some stuff in the car I picked up on the way over. Come give me a hand."

We walked to the car and Clyde opened the trunk, reached in and handed me a pack of flea powder, a jar of de-worming medication and some serious-looking soap that was supposed to kill ticks. We walked to the back yard and I yelled, "Here, Pete."

The dog stood up and looked at us with a slight wag of his tail. We walked up, and Clyde explained how to make dog bread, which he said would be good for the dog and tender on his stomach until he could get on regular Purina Dog Chow.

He also showed me how to apply the tick lotion—let it stay on overnight and then wash Pete in the morning, letting him dry before applying the flea powder. Nothing to it, I thought.

Clyde said goodbye and walked into the house to finish his coffee. Soon after, I heard the Bird start and drive off. It was then that I realized my best summer ever was truly at an end. I didn't know it then, but I would only see Clyde a few more times before I was older and off to college.

But for now, I worked on Pete every day. It wasn't long until I had him in really good shape. No ticks, fleas or ear mites, and he had a good shiny coat. Dog bread, which was cornbread with lots of bacon grease and two eggs that I snuck into the mix, was his morning food and chow in the afternoon.

He went everywhere with me. It was then that I started working on his gun shy problem.

First, I would settle him down and would clap my hands behind his head. He jumped and tried to run. I stayed with the clapping until he would finally sit still, turn his head and just look at me. Then I moved to my .22. I let him smell the gun.

I rubbed him with the wooden stock and the barrel. After a week or so, I would fire the gun. At first, he was really startled and would start shaking and whining. But slowly, he got over noise of the gun and would walk with me down to the pond where I shot several times at once with his leash tied to my belt.

Over time, he stopped being afraid of the noise and smell of gun powder.

Next was the shotgun. Getting used to the loud noise of the shotgun took longer. I shot my 20 gauge until my shoulder hurt before I could get him to calm down. But I finally got him to stay even after a few quick shots. I had him trained.

It had taken me about three weeks, and I was so proud that I called Clyde. He said he'd be heading our way that afternoon.

When he got to the house, I saw he had another dog in the car. He got out and let the dog run, a beautiful, healthy hound, also gun shy. The two dogs met up and started sniffing and playing. I asked, "Where'd that one come from?"

Clyde said, "Lost in the woods, so I brought him home. Good dog. Good lines. I won't have any trouble getting him to a good home. Now how about Pete? I understand you'll to be leaving us soon. What do you plan to do with him?"

"Well, I never thought about that. What do you think I should do?" I asked.

"I got a feller outside of Jackson Landing that is looking for a good bird dog. I told him I might have one. What do you think?" Clyde asked.

I was crushed. All my work and Pete had turned into a fine-looking Pointer. But I knew he was a working dog and needed space to run and time to learn how to hunt. Clyde assured me that the man was good with dogs and that Pete would have a good home.

With my head down, I said ok. I truly understood working dogs and their need to run and chase game.

"You sure he's a good man with bird dogs?" I asked.

Looking at me with mock surprise, he said, "Tommy, would I ever let a man that didn't care for his dogs have a dog you worked so hard to clean up and train? Pete was more a test for you than for him, and, son, you passed with flying colors. Now let's load 'em up before we both get tears in our way."

With the dogs loaded up, Clyde drove past the oleanders down the racetrack road, as Will and I called it, and that part of my life was gone.

***

Two years passed quickly, and my summer visits were not nearly as long as I would have wished. As my father moved our family from base to base, seeking a B-52 Wing or his Star, my life became a seemingly never ending of meeting and gaining new friends, then suddenly uprooting and on to a new military base, new town and new, but short-lived, friends.

I received a call from Robbye during my first year at college inviting me to, as she explained, 'a very special wedding'. She told me that Booty was going to get married to Nell in June of that year, and Clyde wanted Will and I to come to the wedding. The wedding was going to be at the Big House in Greenwood.

Lord, I thought the world has turned upside down. It seemed like the days of no coloreds in the house were truly gone, at least as far as the Fitzhughs were concerned. I was shocked and proud at the same time. "Damn right, we'll be there. Just give me the date, and by the way, who's helping the bride?"

Robbye replied, "Why I am, and your uncle Clyde and Booty's grandfather, Moses, are standing up for Booty, whose legal name is William F. Jones."

"Well, I'll be damned," I said. "I want to see his face when I call him Bill Jones. I truly can't wait. And the wedding's in the Big House?" I exclaimed, still in shock.

Robbye said, "Yes, isn't that the durnest thing you've ever heard? I'm so proud of our aunt and uncle. They've come a long way in this crazy place we all call home."

"Any problem if I stay for the summer. I need a break from this college stuff, and I need some kinda job. Turns out, college is pretty expensive. Oh, and by the way, what's Booty doing for work?" I said.

"Well," Robbye stammered, "that's kind of a long and ugly story. I'll try and keep it brief. Clyde came home after work earlier than usual one afternoon. Booty had been working at the Big House most of the day but had taken a break to go see Nell. You obviously know how sweet Booty is on that gal and little Robert."

"Yeah, I know. How in the world could I ever forget Nell and little Robert? Plus, that's all Booty could talk about the last time I was with him, and now they're getting married. So, go on tell me what happened?"

"Clyde came home early and went to his damn hidey hole wanting a drink, which the doctor told him to lay off because of his heart problem. Well, he couldn't find the damn whiskey. So, he got mad as hell. When Booty showed up for work the next day, Clyde, for some ungodly reason, blamed Booty for stealing the bottle and drinking it all."

"The hell you say! Why Booty never touched a drop of liquor or even hinted at sneaking a beer. Never," I said shocked.

"I know," Robbye anxiously said. "But he and Clyde started arguing, and Booty finally admitted that he'd poured all the whiskey out because he knew Clyde wasn't supposed to be drinking, and Booty thought the hidden bottle was just too much of a temptation. Well, Clyde went half-crazy yelling at Booty, that it wasn't any of his damn business and that he was lying."

"Booty swore he would never lie to Clyde and was only trying to help. Said he loved Clyde, who was the only white man that treated him with respect. But Clyde was enraged. Your uncle, Son, said they were yelling so loud he could hear them all the way at his house. Clyde then started beating on Booty."

I stopped Robbye mid conversation and said, "What the hell? Clyde was beating on Booty about that damn whisky?"

Robbye sounded like she was in tears. "Yes, he started beating on Booty like a wild man. He grabbed some old telephone wire laying by the dog pen and beat Booty on legs until they were bleeding through his pants."

At this point, Robbye was sobbing so much I could hardly understand her. But she continued, "Booty was screaming and crying; finally Clyde stopped. Clyde said it seemed like he came out of a blistering fog."

"Then he broke down and cried; he was sobbing and begging Booty to forgive him, told him he was like a son, and he kept begging that God and Booty would forgive him. He told Booty the pressures of his life that he always hid from others and joked about, plus the craving for a drink must have caused him to snap."

"And, of course, Booty wept, and they held each other for a long time. It was then that Clyde told Booty that as a wedding present he was going to give him the Yellow Bird."

I interrupted again, "He's giving him the Bird? I can't believe it. He loves that car."

Robbye, now composed, replied, "That's why he wanted Booty and Nell to have one of the things that he loved the most. He also told Booty that he had gotten him a job in Baton Rouge with a Coca Cola distributor, who is a friend of Clyde's."

"Booty will start work right after he and Nell are married. That's the story as best I know."

"Well, what exactly will Booty be doing?" I asked.

Robbye replied, "Best I can tell from what Norma said is he will have a route with a driver who will be his immediate boss and will deliver Cokes and other drinks to stores, bars and restaurants. Norma said if he works hard, he could have a good future working for the company. Regardless, Clyde has been very remorseful and has kept all the promises he made."

Still in shock, I replied, "Well, he damn well better keep those promises. Booty has been nothing but good for Clyde and Norma. Why hell, he taught me more during my summers with him than I ever learned from some cockeyed teacher in the schools I had to go to."

"I'll never forget the lessons that both Booty and Clyde taught me. Especially, about blackberry picking," I jokingly said.

Laughing, Robbye replied, "Now, don't be too hard on your old uncle. He loves you and treats you like you are his son. And them girls at Aunt Sue's still ask about that pretty white boy named Tommy."

"Well, I'm still available for berry pickin'," I laughed. "But seriously, all of you have been good to me and good for me. I'm just surprised by the way life twists and turns. You never know what's comin'."

"It's just as if everything went past so quickly. It seems so confusing."

Looking back, I began to think that maybe Uncle Clyde had finally realized he wasn't immortal. Maybe time and life were catching up with him and all that he had ever known was rapidly changing. I think what he really wanted was life in the old South to change for the better before he was gone.

Still on the phone, Robbye waited for my reply. "I'll call my dad, but regardless, we'll be at the wedding. And by the way, please don't forget the summer job," I said.

"No, I won't forget. I know just the place and the right folk," she promised. "You just come down as soon as you can. I love you."

"I love you too. I'll see you soon," I said before hanging up the phone.

I made it down to Greenwood for the big wedding day. My brother, Will, was unfortunately overseas in the Navy in that crazy war. My parents were living in California again, and my dad's job wouldn't let them come to the wedding.

Of course, I went and stayed at the French House since there was a lot of back and forth at the Big House preparing for the wedding. The Big House in Greenwood was decorated with ribbons and flowers. Everyone it seems had worked hard decorating and fixing food for all who were invited.

Moses and Aunt Sue were there. Son, Eva and their two sons, James and Matthew, back from the Army, brought their girlfriends. Ben Cummings sent a gift of $50 in a nice wedding card. Robbye, Ruth and my grandmother all came. My parents sent Booty a $100 as a gift.

A few girls from Aunt Sue's were there. Unfortunately, not Marcie. Aunt Sue made her wonderful lemon pound cake, and as a special treat for me, blackberry cobbler.

The black preacher from the local Baptist church was going to preside. All seemed good in the world that day. And then the telephone rang. Clyde answered, and Ms. Minnie said she had Johnnie Franklin on the phone and that he wanted to talk to Clyde about something very important.

Clyde spoke into the phone saying in a friendly manner, "Hell-o, Johnnie, how you doing this fine day?"

Johnnie, in his deep southern drawl, said, "Well, Clyde, I got about 15 men standing next to me that heard you were having that negra boy of yours get married to some negra gal at your house today. They say they want to ride down to Greenwood and make sure that ain't true. They be right?"

Clyde said in a strong voice, "Nope, those boys are wrong. That couple is getting married inside my house in the front room, and we're about to start."

"Well," Johnnie said, "they aim to make sure it don't happen, so we're about to head your way. You ready for us?"

Clyde laughed loudly into the phone. "Ready? Let me tell you how ready we are for any redneck Klan that enters our town. You know, Johnnie, there ain't but three ways in and out of Greenwood. And I've got them all covered."

Johnnie laughed saying, "Why hell, Clyde, you know that ain't gonna keep us out. Not 15 or more men?"

Laughing, Clyde said, "Hells fire, Johnnie, we ain't aiming to keep you out; we're aiming to keep you in. You see Matthew, Son's youngest boy, just got out of the Army. And it so happened that a good friend of his at the Army supply depot had a lot of extra equipment he wanted to share with Matthew for a few hundred dollars."

"So Matthew called me, and I told him to load up. You never know when you may need military-type equipment. We got us about 15 carbines, 12 M-1 rifles, three Browning Automatic rifles. Damn things will put a hole through both sides of a car with one shot; hell of a gun."

"And for an extra fifty bucks, the guy threw in a box of 20 hand grenades, plus enough ammunition to start a real war. So, the idea is to get you inside and block your way out and blow your men down if they cause any trouble. You do fully understand, right?"

Johnnie was stone silent as all his fellow Klan's men surrounding him waited impatiently for the word to go. "Yep, I think I understand, Clyde. Sounds good to me. Now how are you going to get me out of this mess with all these folk standing around anxious for a showdown?" Johnnie asked nervously.

Clyde stroked his chin in thought and then said, "You know, Johnnie, I've been stopping at your hamburger joint ever since you opened. Ain't that right?"

Johnnie said, "Sure have. You've always been a good customer and a good friend until the Klan started harassing these colored folk."

It was at that moment that Clyde knew he really had him cornered. Johnnie never said 'colored folk', so he was hanging on to Clyde for help. "Can you hang on a minute? Norma is waving at me," said Clyde.

Norma said, "Get off the damn phone? The wedding is about to start?"

Clyde replied, "I'm talking to the governor. Tell everyone Governor Davis sends his best wishes and is sending a state trooper to take the couple to Baton Rouge for their honeymoon."

"Alright, Clyde; what's your plan?" Johnnie asked.

"Johnnie, I'm going to make sure you get all the concession rights to all baseball games, black and white, in the Louisiana league for the next five years. And, if that works out, I'll help you get into Tiger stadium. At the local games, you'll be the only one selling food and drinks. But you gotta sell to colored and white at the same prices, no short selling."

Stunned by the offer, Johnnie said, "You can do that, Clyde?"

"Yessir. I just got off the phone with the Governor Jimmie Davis and he said if you, Johnnie, swore off the Klan, the concession rights are yours."

"If you can do that, Clyde, you got a deal. And you can tell your army to go home and my best to the bride and groom."

"Done and done," said Clyde. "But keep that loud mouth Henry out. Agreed?"

"Done and done" said Johnnie. "We'll talk soon."

Clyde hung up the phone, walked into the main parlor and shouted, "Who's getting married and when does the party start?"

I eased over to Clyde and said, "Do you really have all that military equipment, and were you talking to the governor?"

Clyde looked at me and said, "Mama had a lot of ugly kids but not any dumb ones."

When the ceremony started, Clyde and Moses stood beside Booty. Little Robert was the ring bearer and walked up to Moses giving him the ring for Booty to put on Nell's finger. Norma gave a bouquet of flowers to Nell. It was all so very touching – white folk and black folk coming together to celebrate life.

Luke Faucheux had donated a few bottles of champagne and some new-fangled beer from Holland called Heineken. We all visited and talked about the past. Everyone laughed about my blackberry adventures. Actually, the whole party felt strange to me as I stood looking out the window while drinking a beer and smoking a Lucky.

Booty wandered over and said, "Tommy, you feeling ok? You look like you lost your best friend."

I turned to him and said, "I have lost my best friend, but I lost him to a beautiful woman with a fine-looking son. But I feel like we've lost each other. I'll never have a friend better than you."

Tears came to both of us as we hugged, and Booty said, "Tommy, you will always be with me. You and Mr. Clyde done knew my wife afore I ever knew her. You both protected me from those outlaw men."

"You see, Tommy, we will be together forever and ever. No matter where you be, I'll know you be with me. That's what friends, true friends, be all about."

I looked at Booty and said, "No truer words be spoken. I'll always remember you and hope with all my heart that you and Nell are always well and safe. Speaking of your bride, where is she?"

Booty turned and looked over his shoulder, "Nell, c'mon over here and visit with Tommy and me."

Nell walked shyly over to where Booty and I were standing. I looked at her and said, "You're a beautiful bride. Now tell me how happy you are being loved by so many people that a few years ago, you didn't even know existed?"

Nell smiled and said, "Why, Tommy, you was one of the first white people to ever talk kindly to me. You, Ms. Robbye and Ms. Ruth always be good, and I promise I never forget all that kindness."

"Well, you are a very lucky and special young woman. You two will always be with me as friends and fond memories. I still remember the first day we met. Nell, do you remember?"

Nell looked startled but then smiled as she said, "Why, course I member. How could a body ever forget Ms. Ruth and her big ol gun?"

We all laughed as Booty said, "Lordy, lordy, who don shot shorty?"

I was taking a drink of a beer when he said that, and I laughed so hard that I could hardly swallow. I had to wipe my face as I said, "Well, this has been the nicest and most fun I've had since I started coming here; just look at all these people laughing and talking." Booty and Nell both smiled as Nell said, "And, yes, we still loves you 'Blackberry Boy'."

Booty, in a deep voice sounding like Clyde, said, "We gotcha, didn't we?"

We were all still laughing when Uncle Son meandered over to us and said, "Well now, I can finally shave in peace with you two horse's asses gone."

We kept laughing and noticed Son was drinking champagne. I said, "Uncle Son, what are you doing with champagne? You shouldn't be drinking."

He made a harrumph sound saying, "Why, hell, I hate this sparkly stuff, I'm just holding the glass until I can find a place to pour it out."

"Just throw it in the yard; no one will notice," I suggested.

Son said, "I thought it might kill Norma's ferns, and I'd never hear the end of that. But she ain't lookin', is she?"

Nell looked before saying, "No, sir, Mr. Son."

"Well, then," Son said, "here goes." And he threw the champagne through the screen of the open window in the parlor. Booty, Nell and I started laughing so hard that Norma looked our way. Son looked at us grinned and hollered, "Congratulations to the bride and groom."

Everyone joined in the congratulations as Son slyly walked over to talk to his sister, my grandmother. She got on him good. "Son, why do you still act like a child? You and your crazy shenanigans never cease to embarrass me."

Son replied, "Now, hold on there, Elsie. A famous philosopher once said, and I shall quote, 'Genius is the ability to recall childhood at will'. That's me and always will be. I like being who I am. I like watching people be happy."

"Hell, Big Sister, I want to live forever and recall my rostabout childhood whenever I need a boost. Now, give me a much-needed hug, and don't tell Norma about the sparkly juice."

They hugged for a long time, with my grandmother laughing and saying quite loud, "Son, it's a wonder you can still remember anything, much less your ramblin' days."

Time was pushing on; twilight was near when Louisiana State Trooper Melvin pulled into the driveway got out of his patrol car and sternly announced, "I'm here to pick up the Jones wedding party and escort them to Baton Rouge."

All the people of color froze. Then Clyde walked up to Melvin and they both started laughing. Clyde walked over to Booty and looked Booty square in the eye and said, "Gotcha one last time."

We all toasted Mr. Bill Jones and his wife, Nell, as Clyde said, "Aunt Sue will now sing a song for the bride and groom and for all of us still standing."

Everyone chuckled at Clyde's little joke. Then Aunt Sue started to sing in a loud, but proud, voice, "God Bless America, land that I love."

Everyone stopped talking and stood perfectly still. Trooper Melvin removed his cap, as did all the others black or white, and put their hand over their heart and joined in with the blessed song of the majesty of our nation.

And then it was time to call it a day-time for everyone to part company. We all crowded onto the front porch as Booty and Nell walked to their new car covered with 'just married' signs. State Trooper Melvin led the way out of town. Robbye and Norma wept.

Clyde's tears on his cheek were quickly wiped away, and then he yelled, "Let's all go down to the Monteleore."

But those days were also gone. As we watched the two cars travel down the highway, we all silently hoped times were changing. Clyde had found a little house in Baton Rouge that Booty, Nell and little Robert could call home. Clyde and Norma paid the first six months of rent as an additional wedding present.

All was peaceful, yet exciting. As everyone was leaving, I decided it was time for a real drink. I walked toward the back of the house to the kitchen and there sat Ruth with a large Canadian club and Ginger Ale, slowly beginning to feel no pain.

She said, with a bit of a slur, "Never thought I'd see the day that two colored folk would get married in this house. But things do change in this crazy thing of life. '

I looked at her and simply said, "All things change. Sometimes good sometimes bad. Today was a good day. Change today was good. Now please pour your sweet nephew a good drink, heavy on the Canadian Club, light on the Ginger Ale."

Ruth looked at me saying as she poured, "A strong one for a strong philosopher." We toasted and both drank big.

Ruth said, "To our future, Tommy. May the good times be many and sad times be few."

During my last summer in Jackson Landing, Luke Faucheux got me a job in a 'bomb factory'. The Vietnam war was going full tilt. Small but lethal ammunition factories were popping up all over the country. So why not Jackson Landing?

In the 'Bum' factory, as Clyde called it, we made these little round steel balls.

Years later, I found out we were making anti-personnel bombs. Dropped from planes, the bombs scattered amongst the jungle and killed or wounded God knows how many people. I wasn't proud of that. It still haunts me. Ugly stuff.

But hell, no one knew a damn thing about that mess of a war. I worked hard $1.75 per hour. Hard work but I liked the people. I was the only white person in the damn bum factory.

I got to spend several days with Clyde. We drove up to Northwood to get burgers, and I noticed how the place was dressed up and looked like a real restaurant instead of a local hang out. Johnnie met us inside at the bar and said, "Drinks and burgers on me."

He looked straight at me and said, "Your uncle Clyde saved my life and made life better for my family. I just wanted you to know, Tommy, you come from good stock. *A* man who keeps his word is hard to find, but Clyde Fitzhugh is that type of man."

Clyde sarcastically said, "Pretty speech, Johnnie. Now, where's my Grapette and cheeseburger."

They both laughed patted each other on the back and Johnnie said, "Comin' right up."

I looked hard at Clyde for a moment then asked, "How is it you always came to this place knowing that Johnnie, and probably half the folk in here, were Klan?"

Clyde looked around and said, "Yeah, you're 'bout right on that count. But you should always remember something Tommy, keep your friends close but your enemies closer. You see, I know these folk. I know the gooduns and the bad."

"I listen and I remember whose ass may need kicking and whose back may need stroking. I stroked Johnny's back, and he'll always remember that and I'll always remember the times he was against me. Now he owes me. He will be with me when and if I need him. Remember, you rather have him inside your tent pissing out than outside pissing in."

A stark lesson I've never forgotten. Clyde knowingly smiled and said, "Now, let's enjoy these cheeseburgers."

Life went on for me. I returned to college and worked hard through several summer sessions to graduate on time, but I sorely missed the warm and crazy times of the Louisiana summers. I missed Clyde, Norma, Booty, Robbye, Ruth, my grandmother and my brother, Will, who was still in the Navy sailing around the world.

Fond memories remained of the blackberry patch, morning coffee and brandy, Lucky Strikes and the adventures of youth. But the clock never stops ticking. Time moved on for us all.

1969

I was very fortunate to get into a pretty good university. Luck was with me. I had a great counselor who guided me through applications, SAT exams and extracurricular activities. She pushed hard for me to get enrolled and I made it.

My roommate was my best friend from high school. I made it all the way through, he didn't. He ended up in Nam, forever changing his carefree life. He wandered lost for a while found a good woman and settled. He remains my close friend to this day, forty-eight years later.

I'm pretty sure it was a Thursday night. It was as cold as the Midwest can be in the dead of winter, which was damn cold. I was standing in my dormitory room looking out of the room's large picture window toward the Cushman Motor Factory. Snow was gently falling.

The phone in the hall rang. Someone answered and asked for my roommate. He got up from his bed put out one of his never-ending cigarettes and went to the phone. He walked back into the room and said, "Tom, I've got some bad news. I think you need to go to the phone."

I turned walked to the phone booth in the hall and said, "Hello."

"Tommy, this is your dad. Robbye called a while ago and asked me to call and talk to you."

He hesitated as I said, "Yes."

Dad said, "Clyde died last night."

We both paused. My dad continued, "He went through some new surgery called a by-pass on his heart and he didn't make it."

I didn't know what to say.

"The funeral is tomorrow," my dad continued. "And we don't think you should try and make it. The weather is awful. I wanted you to know that Clyde went out of the world as he would have wished – quiet and peaceful."

"Norma is taking it well. And we all know you would be there, but I really think it best that you stay in school. The blizzard you are getting isn't letting up."

I couldn't talk. My throat closed in anguish. The tears started. The memories came back in waves. I simply said, "I love you, Dad; I love all of you."

My dad replied, "I know, Tom, I know. We all love you. Take care, son. We'll call soon."

I walked back to my room. My roommate saw my tears and said, "Sorry, Tom. I'll leave you alone for a while. Ok?"

"Sure, thanks," I said. I lit a Lucky Strike. I looked out the window. In a flash, I thought of all I loved about my family. The pride I really had for my father, mother and the entire Fitzhugh family.

And then I thought about what our country was going through.

I'd seen the Kennedys die, the Selma march, Martin Luther King Jr.'s death, Medgar Evers, the young freedom riders brutally murdered in Mississippi, the Birmingham bombings, the rise of nationalism though the campaign of George Wallace, the snide racist remarks of a certain type of uncaring students, the furor of the Vietnam war.

Life I thought, *What was this all about if not the cry of our souls.*

I lost track of Booty. I never found the black girl I had a crush on, and I never ate a cheeseburger better than the one I ate with Booty the day Clyde stood down the Klan. But I never lost my feeling of sorrow for my fellow man and for that I have to thank my mother, father, brothers, Aunt Robbye, and most importantly, Clyde Fitzhugh. The Big House is no longer standing but the long, hot Louisiana summers remain.

***

I would like to express my admiration and fascination for the authorship and lives of Ernest Hemingway, John Steinbeck, Tennessee Williams Jim Harrison, A.E. Proulx, William Styron, William Faulkner, Zora Neal Hurston, Bob Dylan, David Mallett, John Prine, Kurt Vonnegut, James Baldwin, Fredrick Douglas, Dr. Martin Luther King and countless others.

And Finally

The events and people depicted in this fictional story are in many ways non-fictional. Much of my life revolved around the lives of those I wrote about. Most of the experiences written were actual, to a degree and contrary to what many readers may assume I truly loved my life in Louisiana.

I have so many people to thank for their encouragement to continue when I often became blocked. But it's done. I hope you enjoyed reading the adventures of a young boy growing toward manhood.

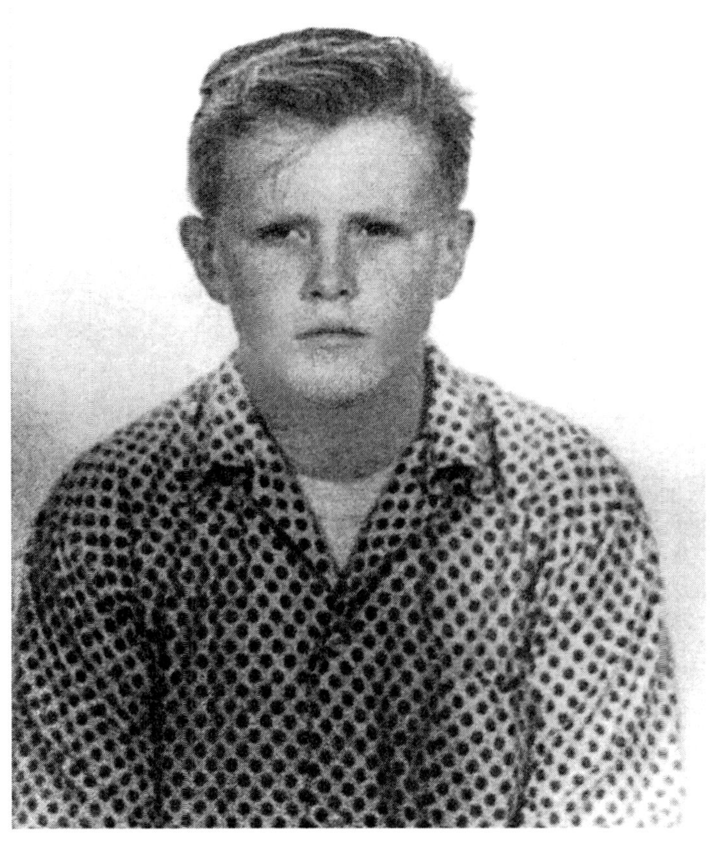

OMG

The greenish Atlantic Ocean churned with criss-crossing waves from a passing summer storm. The normally placid sea had thrown its gut full of man-made garbage onto the beach like the purge from a hung over kid after a spring break drunk. Yellow and green seaweed mixed with the occasional dead fish or bird intermingled with mankind's plastic residue.

Fishing gear and the occasional buoy thrown overboard or casually dumped at sea added a bit more color to the entrails of a neglected ocean. Rip-tide signs had been posted. Too rough and filthy for a swim or even a comforting wade.

My wife, granddaughter and I had come to the Atlantic coast of Florida for a quick vacation get away before the start of school.

It was a swell place we had rented. A nice condo on the beach that was complete with restaurants, bars and loads of activities and adventures for the kids.

Unfortunately, the weather resembled springtime in London rather than the beaches of south Florida. But it was my job to make sure we would have fun in the scarce but hopeful sunshine. I wanted to make sure we would get a chance to enjoy the pool, the food, drinks and finally relax after a grinding year of responsibility and work.

After a pleasant but careful walk on the beach and a thorough examination of several dead fish and birds by my granddaughter, she decided we should make haste and escape to the heated swimming pool complete with a gigantic water slide.

I quickly agreed, thinking why not? The pool area had a great little tiki bar complete with a cute bartender in a string bikini. As I had emphatically explained to my wife, it was a margarita kind of day.

Off to the pool and of course the giant serpentine water slide. My granddaughter was enamored with the durn thing. First out of fear, then after some strong coaxing from my wife and I, her fear became utter delight.

But first came the ritual arrangement of deck chairs of who sat where. I selected the lounge chair closest to the tiki bar while my wife and granddaughter positioned their chairs to get what sun they could through the clouded sky. As soon as the towels were carefully placed, the granddaughter was in the pool.

Quickly, the cry and laughter arose with squeals of 'Papa, get in the pool, please'.

"Give me a few minutes," I replied as I quickly made my way to the lovely young girl tending bar.

I decided to indulge in a double and requested another shot of Patron be added to my margarita. Soon after half of my island elixir had made its way to my incorrigible tummy, I again heard the plea, "Papa jump in," and so I did. A nice cannon ball that sparked the delight of my granddaughter and irritated the tanned lizard like adults sitting by the edge of the pool.

Oh well, I was determined to have fun and the onlookers needed to lighten up. We were here to cut loose and enjoy the surroundings I had dearly paid for.

The tequila was mixing well with the bloody Mary I drank while waiting for my salmon omelet at the food trough also known as the breakfast buffet. My spirits were definitely rising.

Granddaughter, after all the begging, had swam off to make friends with some other kids in the pool. She met three other little girls and they all seemed to be playing well together.

So I swam across the pool and did several laps to loosen up the old back. The warm water felt great and the exercise created a welcome stretch relieving all the anxiety and tension from my aging body.

I stopped in the shallow end and watched the kids take turns doing handstands. They each struggled to the bottom of the shallow end of the pool and tried to do hand stands with their legs kicking wildly above the water.

Of course our little 6-year-old wanting to fit in as she tried her best to hold her breath and gain her balance, but couldn't quite hold her breath long enough while under water to get the balance in check. I figured she would get the hang of the balancing issue, so I climbed the steps out of the pool and headed for my margarita which I downed quickly, turned and headed for the tiki bar.

My wife spoke up with a sarcastic 'Don't you think you've had enough'.

To which I replied, "If I did, I wouldn't be getting another."

Boy did that piss her off. Oh well. I was enjoying myself regardless of the weather or the overly tanned elderly couples lounging like lizards at poolside.

The lovely young lady at the tiki bar happily refurbished my drink. We made some idle chitchat then she gave cute smile as she looked slyly at the tip jar at the end of the bar. I left her a couple of bucks as she said, "Thanks and the next one is on the house."

Smiling like a hot dog beach boy, I pulled in my gut as I walked back to my beach chair to bake in what little sun peeped through the clouds. Soon I heard a little voice yelling, "Papa, please jump in the pool."

I took a slug of the margarita, jumped into the pool with a miserable but effective cannon ball again, aggravating all the sedated adults sitting close to the pool's edge.

I awaited further instructions from my granddaughter and they came fast. "Papa, can you help me with my hand stand?"

"Sure," I replied.

With a little help from me, she was able to master the leg-swinging breath holding handstand. I had never seen her so excited.

"I did it, I did it, now you, Papa. You do it."

With a little more coaxing, I finally agreed to attempt the handstand.

Now for a 65-year-old man, this was going to be no easy task. But as I said we were here to have fun and if fun was to get grandpa to try and do a handstand in the pool, then so be it.

I'd give it a solid attempt.

I sucked in all the air possible, held my breath and wildly kicked as I desperately reached for the bottom of the pool. I was successful as I waved my legs around in the air. My sense of pride was evident as I surfaced to the shouts from my granddaughter.

"Yea, Papa, you did it, you did it." I was tickled to see her so thrilled by my less than stellar but determined athletic ability.

However, seeing my wife's scornful look was a different matter. She stared at me with a scowling expression I hadn't witnessed since I missed our 30th wedding anniversary.

I noticed that all the kids in the pool were smirking, laughing and pointing at me while parents stared. Some of the men looked with laughing grins. The women were whispering with disdain as they glanced at my wife who modestly maintained a serious scowl of embarrassment.

I thought what the heck is this all about. I just did a simple handstand in the shallow end of the pool.

I climbed the steps out of the pool and walked toward my chair as my wife's glassy stare quickly melted away all the pride I had earned for such an act of athletic ability.

As I tentatively walked toward my assigned deck chair my wife hissed at me, "Your bathing suit has no inside webbing."

"Yeah so what?" I said as I casually picked up my drink.

"So what, smart ass, I'll tell you so what. When you stood on your hands, your bathing suit slipped down and you exposed your naked self for the whole world to see!"

"Oh my God," I said. I quickly put my drink on the table and walked away from the shouts of 'Please, Papa, do it again'.

As I quick walked to our condo I kept repeating, **Oh my God.**

MR. TRANH

The first time I saw Son Tranh, he was standing in the middle of a dirt road that led to what would soon become home for both of us for the next ten days. Although, we had never met, we both had enrolled in a silent Zen meditation program at an Ashram in southern Georgia.

Son was short in stature but his arms were those of a man well acquainted with hard labor.

He was speaking in broken English to a man slender but sinewy in build whose arms were covered with multi colored tattoos. Skin artwork commonly referred to as 'sleeves'. The man's shaved head was balanced with a slight white beard and the stark white pate of his slick baldness.

At this time, I had no idea Son would become not only a close friend but also my mentor during my stay at the Zen meditation center.

Our choice was to refrain from the noise, chaos and any communication with the so-called 'modern world' for ten uninterrupted days. Or plead to go home.

After deciding, with great trepidation to attempt this oncoming lark, I decided to sign on for the ten-day retreat.

A friend had recommended the 'challenge' while he and I were skiing in Utah two years prior. Initially, it was a simple bet of 'you couldn't make it'. It had taken me two years to gain the fortitude to attempt something I knew nothing about.

But I wanted to give it a try. I thought maybe the experience would stir my soul and give me some welcome relief from my stressful life.

My friend described the meditation program and assured me that it was only ten days of what was called 'noble silence', or simply no talking. Additionally, required was a vegetarian diet which absolutely petrified me with visions of gray warm oatmeal for breakfast, lentils and kale or some semblance for dinner (lunch).

And of course, no telephones of any sort and absolutely no computer laptops or iPad. Paper and pencil ok, but no mail. Cut off from civilization. In the boonies of Georgia.

Initially, I thought there had to be some way to contact the outside world but if I couldn't abide the rules of the retreat, I could always leave.

I visualized freaking out, abandoning my temporary home at the center making a mad dash to my car and rushing back to the civilized cacophony I initially wished to escape.

I looked up the retreat on my computer and found that my stay would also require group meditation for a minimum of 4 hours each day. Jeez, 4 hours a day for ten days. Plus, additional voluntary sittings throughout the day.

I decided to dig deeper and check out the website and see what others who had been to the retreat thought of their experiences and what might be revealed to a novice.

Most responses were positive but a few were, to put it mildly, pretty far out there.

One woman was antic as she described 'mind control and celibacy'. Another described the facilities as a 'concentration camp with horrid food'. Both seemed on the verge of a breakdown as they related their experiences on a video camera, obviously smuggled into the Ashram.

The visuals were poor quality, but boy, could these women talk some bad trash.

I read more reviews and most were upbeat and overall positive in content and sounded sane. I thought two negatives and about ten positive? I might as well give it a go. I'd been through military boot camp so this should work out fine.

I made my reservations and signed up as a new student. My friend had called my upcoming experience, "Zen boot camp."

I told my wife about my decision and she accepted it with, "Sure you want to do this? And if you're really going, remember it's ten days of silence and fasting."

I smugly replied, "Yeah, I can do this. If I can't make the ten days, I'll just head back home."

Relenting, she said, "OK, but I don't want to find out that you're actually heading to Savannah for a week long lark with some of your so called buds."

Defending my honor, I said, "Now there's no way that's going to happen. Besides, I really think this may be good for me. I'm taking this seriously. No messing around, I promise."

I'd never meditated for any significant amount of time. People from all walks of life talk the meditation lingo but not meditation for 4 or more hours a day. I mean who meditates for that long except some creepy swami in India?

Why had I decided to subject myself to these rules I was informed would be strictly enforced? I thought I couldn't make it for two days much less ten. But quitting like a total cop out was definitely not in the cards.

Of course, I continued to dream up excuses. I thought, *Hell I've done my share of sacrifice and tested my physical abilities throughout my life.*

However, I had gracefully aged and become a more mature man (I like that description) who looked forward to a double Hendricks gin martini accompanied with a porterhouse steak cooked Pittsburgh style, accompanied with a healthy order of pommes frites, of course at a great steak joint in The City.

Topping off my memory menu with a California Cabernet from Nickel & Nickel.

But reasoning barked a strong NO, I was determined to complete this program, if for no other reason to prove to myself that I still had the stuff. Say what? Well, I wasn't getting any younger and I did need a serious break from society, work, family and friends and well, you can probably guess the rest of my concerns.

So now I found myself driving to Georgia and the ten days of perceived torture as I continued to concentrate and say to myself over and over, "I can do this."

But occasionally, that little creep called self-doubt would light up the brain cells and ask, "What the hell was a zen retreat doing in BF Georgia anyway? Why would some screwball put a retreat or monastery out in the middle of a pine tree forest?"

Rationalizing, my business brain kicked in as I thought, *Oh yeah-cheap land and volunteer labor. The successful business plan of every great religion or political philosophy.*

I thought I had my potential retreat tenure all figured out. If I didn't like the place, I would quietly leave and head to a city like Savannah. Yep, it was on my mind. I mentally blamed my wife for putting the idea into my sly little brain.

What a lame excuse. My lovely wife was justifiably concerned about my previous traveling adventures.

But ah, Savannah, great food nice nightlife, cute young ladies looking to have fun. Then came that blast of balance to my brain, "Shut the hell up. You're going to complete this program slow down and find your inner self."

I admit I had been tilting toward the wrong side of life's highway. Intense pressure from work, family in turmoil, questions of existence, no self-respect after so many questionable business deals, or as my mother described them 'monkey business'. I needed the break, and this was the path I had decided to follow.

Gee, I thought, *I'm sounding positively zen like already.*

Upon arrival at the Ashram, I checked in at the administrative offices and got the basic run down about where I would sleep and eat.

Then I was forced to surrender the keys to my new BMW and give up my iPhone. I hesitated on both requests from the very cute young lady behind the reception desk.

"It's required," she calmly said.

Standing in front of her feeling naked without my phone and my car keys, my mind began to playfully wander to its disturbing thoughts, "I wonder if she's good in the sack? I wonder if she might have a drink with me after the ten days of torture were over?"

As my mind again drifted to an invigorating rest at the Ritz Carlton concierge floor, a handsome young man walked up and introduced himself. He then turned to his lovely wife, the serene well-mannered woman who was the receptionist at a Zen Monastery and gave her a healthy kiss.

So much for the Ritz.

The young lady directed me to the cottage I would call home for my ten-day forced solitude. The negative thoughts of 'what the hell am I doing here?' stayed locked to the cerebral part of my slightly abused brain. I knew I had to somehow complete this experience of ten-day meditative requirements while remaining sane.

How? Was the question.

Son, my soon to be roommate, the Vietnamese guy that had been standing in the driveway listening and smiling at the tall lanky pale bald white dude who was still waving his skinny, heavily tattooed arms, expressing in a high-pitched elevated southern twang, "The goal of meditation is perfection. And the way to perfection is through meditation and silence."

Which he maintained was, "A means of enhancing inner reflection thus helping one reach a state of perfection."

Son, listened intently, his head cocked to one side with a look of confusion as the guy yammering, whose name I later learned was Clive, continued his theory of meditation.

Son kept saying, "I know, Mr. Clive, and yes, I understand meditation but how you get perfection, how you get to a state of Nirvana?"

Clive responded somewhat patiently, "You work at it; you meditate then you reflect on your thoughts and cleanse your body of mindless irrational thoughts. You stop the monkey mind from wandering."

Becoming irritated, Son said, "You not calling me monkey, are you?"

Somewhat exasperated Clive posed in namaste while saying, "No that's simply an expression meaning to slow your random thought process. Slow your thinking, anticipate nothing. Cast your thoughts to a state of nothingness."

Son put his hands together in prayer fashion and said, "Namaste," as he backed away. Apparently, he'd heard enough.

I thought the entire conversation sounded a bit simplistic, and later found that after the lecture from Clive, Son was more confused than me.

As Clive walked away, he turned and said loudly, "Now you give it a good try you hear," as if the louder he spoke the better to communicate with Son. Typical.

Moments later, as I was unloading my personal gear from my car, I again heard Son speaking briskly, in what I assumed was Vietnamese, to someone on his cell phone. Obviously, we had not started the 'noble silence' yet.

I continued unloading my car and couldn't help but overhear the conversation, which ended abruptly as Son said in broken English, "Bye Bye, I call you later. Take care of business and don't forget pay bills."

Another voice broke my thought process as a bullhorn squealed loudly and announced, "Everyone please proceed to the meeting hall for the first and final orientation meeting. All rules and regulations will be explained at the orientation."

"If you haven't turned in your car keys, iPhone, computer laptops, please bring them with you. They will be secured and returned after your stay."

I quickly stashed my backpack in the room I had been assigned.

The guy on the bullhorn continued making the announcement several more annoying times.

Looking through the one window in my room, I noticed a large group of men from separate living quarters begin walking in the same direction. Since I had no idea where the meeting hall was, I decided I'd just follow the crowd.

Off to a weak start I thought as we straggled along the path to the meeting hall. *How strange,* I thought, *we were, supposedly, all here seeking peace, contentment or whatever from society at large yet here we were mindlessly following the 'crowd' to somewhere.*

We approached a simple but well-designed building, which was apparently the meeting hall.

Entering, we walked to a large office area that was lined with folding chairs. Women on one side of the room and men on the other. Yes, there were women but you were allowed no discussion or eye contact with them.

The 'old students' those that had been through the program and the 'teachers' took this very seriously or so it seemed at the time.

Orientation was brief but well organized.

We were instructed that this would be the last time we could speak for the ten-day program, unless asked a question or were reproached by a teacher.

The head teacher dressed as a Buddhist monk in a cloak of orange asked, "Any questions?" There were a few but most were very basic.

The teacher continued in serious fashion saying, "Soon we will begin Noble Silence. There is to be no talking, no gestures, minimal eye contact and no signals from one to another. No communication whatsoever. Just noble silence."

"You will be awakened at 4am. Lights out at 9pm. You are required to attend 4 group meditation sessions and at least 1 voluntary sitting during the day. If you oversleep, an old student will come wake you. In the group meditation, if you fall asleep, you will be awakened."

"Remember, you are here to meditate and extinguish all thoughts of reality. To do that, you must strive for equanimity. Only through serious meditation can you achieve this. And finally, have all of you turned in your car keys, iPhone, and computer laptops?"

"If not, you are required to turn them in now and will be given a receipt to have them returned at the end of your sabbatical. Also, no books, reading or writing material. Understood?" Everyone nodded yes. No words, just nods.

The modern world for all of us existed just a few short miles down the road but we were here to become calm, quiet and meditative. Hopefully, to become insightful and find our inner strengths as well weaknesses during our stay in the Georgia woods.

You will be awaken each morning for your first sitting by a gong carried through the Center by an old student. We will breakfast at 6am. Do not be late for any meals. Do not be late for group sittings.

"Respect others and ensure that you observe the Noble Silence. Now you may stand bow and leave for your assigned cottage. The first sitting today will begin at 4pm."

Very intimidating when you thought about it. And I did.

Later that day, I discovered that somehow Son had not given up his phone or car keys.

It didn't seem quite right being required to give up total freedom but I had decided to try and abide by the rules.

Later, I learned that Son had a similar feeling but justified his phone and car keys for his business. So that was that This silence experience was already becoming a bit awkward.

After orientation was complete, an old student walked with us to our cottage. He wore a nametag that said 'Leonard'.

Leonard answered a few basic questions like 'Where's the bathroom, when can we shower and is Noble Science required in the showers?'

The guy that asked about the showers got a nervous laugh from all of us. It was somewhat awkward.

But Leonard sternly replied, "Yes, Noble Silence is to be honored at all times."

We settled in at our respective cottage and prepared for our first group meditation sitting. I didn't have a clue what a group sitting was but thought I'll just follow along.

We had been given rules that would govern our lives for the next ten days and we were expected to honor them. Of course silence being the most noble requirement was to be most respected.

I remembered that lights out was at 9:00pm. And that a large gong carried by Leonard would wake us at 4am with first voluntary meditative sitting at 4:30. Breakfast was at 6am. Then the first mandatory group sitting at 7am. A resting break then the second sitting at 9am, then dinner.

A large group sits from 2pm to 3pm then break for a little rest or more meditation until supper of tea and fruit. Groups sit from 7pm to 9pm then lights out.

I could see this was to be no pleasure cruise. I felt like I did the first day of military boot camp, dazed and confused, yet very anxious to know what would come next.

The cottage I was assigned to had 6 separate rooms with 2 students per room. Bathrooms and showers were nice and clean. *More of the boot camp philosophy,* I thought.

After returning to my assigned room, I busied myself trying to establish some space that would allow me to begin my withdrawal into the inner sanctum of my well-worn noggin.

Organizing a separate living space in the small room was somewhat complicated but possible.

There was a small bunk bed. A writing table and one chair. Since I was there, first I took the bottom bunk. I set my backpack against the wall and carefully placed some personal items on the small table and under my bunk.

Son walked into the room and casually said, "Hi, I take top, I like top. You don't mind but I fart? I have stomach problem. You know where bathroom is?"

I held back my laughter and pointed to my left.

Son said, "Thank you" as he threw his things on the top bunk, turned, bowed and walked out of the room.

I thought, *Well so much for this guy and noble silence. And why the fart thing?*

He returned to the room and casually looked through his bag, pulled out his phone and placed it next to the pillow on the upper bunk. He looked at me and said, "It my alarm. You need?" I shook my head no and smiled.

Son smiled back with a mischievous look on his face. He knew he would soon make me his official co-conspirator.

Many friends have asked after my retreat, "What was the hardest part of the program; the no talking?" "The vegetarian diet of two meals per day?" "No booze?" "No reading or writing?" "What was the most difficult?"

I pause and say, "The greatest difficulty was meditating 4 to 6 hours per day. That was very hard. A significant struggle for a novice to sit with your eyes closed with your mindless thoughts literally out of control for an hour is exceedingly difficult."

"It takes a few hard, really hard days getting used to the rigors of sitting still for an hour. You don't believe me? Try it."

To those that persist their questions, I tell them, "Meditation is not thinking of nothing."

I often repeat the words of the great Leonard Cohen, who after ten years of meditation and following the path of Buddhism, was asked what he had learned as a Buddhist monk. He said, "Nothing." He was right. Nothingness is Nirvana. The mind being still, unthinking.

Earlier at the orientation, the headmaster told us, "You will experience some very difficult days during your demanding meditative experience. Very hard days. Typically, day 2 and day 6 will be your most difficult. So prepare yourself."

"Also, some of you will be required to spend at least one session during the day meditating in a private cell."

I thought 'WHAT?'

He then described the dimensions of the cell as we all sat anxiously apprehensive.

"The individual cell is a cubicle about 4 feet wide 6 feet high and 6 feet long with a single, clerestory window and two cushions to sit. It is an honor to be chosen. It will encourage a deep meditative experience that will enhance your life as well as your strength through meditation."

Not to me it wouldn't. I am claustrophobic and the thought of the cell itself scared the hell out of me.

Surely, I wouldn't be selected for such an advanced contemplative meditation experience.

The teachers voice then boomed as he said, "First sitting is one hour from now. Get settled and be at the meeting hall at the ringing of the meditation hall bell."

Later, after we adjourned to our rooms, Son who had already broken 'Noble Silence' explained that he was an old pro at meditation. He had been practicing meditation for a long time. I thought he would know about the cell thing but finding the right time to ask would be difficult.

I desperately needed to get some reassurance that a novice would never be selected for such torture. I thought I'd be a screaming wild man if selected.

But reassurance from Son would have to wait. We were due for our first sitting and he was still getting his room space in order. The gong rang announcing first sitting. Son and I walked quietly to the meditation hall.

The hall was divided into four separate areas. One for the male students, one for women, one for old male students and one for old female students. We were instructed by the teacher to select our cushion or sitting area arranged in rows along the floor. The room was dimly lit and was actually quite comforting.

We were seated and again lectured on the rules that must be followed during our stay at the retreat.

Then we listened to some Buddhist music, singing bowls, sitars all with a definite soothing sound.

After about 10 minutes, the music stopped and meditation began.

Man, was I freaked out. But also pretty enamored with the thought, *I was here.* I had actually made it.

After that first group sitting, my legs were unbelievably numb. Numb to the point that they would not straighten on their own. I had to pry them straight with my hands.

And to think, this was just the first sitting. I had many more to go over the next ten days.

At the completion of the first sitting, somehow I managed to get my balance and courage to approach the teacher carefully trying not to fall. I bowed courteously and asked if during future sittings I could sit with my back against the meeting room wall.

The teacher instructed me to kneel. He then quietly asked, "For what reason?"

Kneeling on the hard wood floor in pain in front of the master teacher, I explained my leg ordeal.

He stared at me intently and said, "Return to your sitting pad. During the next sittings, you may stretch your legs 3 times during the hour meditation." He stared at me as my mind wanted to scream.

But I thought if the others in the class could do it so could I. Boy, what a downer.

I stood brought my hands together bowed and walked back to my cushion. I straightened my area, fluffed my pillow walked out of the meeting hall to the covered porch area where I found my flip-flops.

I made my way to my room. I began to think that maybe I had really made a mistake coming to this place. My mind was signaling panic. As I walked into my room, I found Son sitting on the top bunk hands folded, back straight looking out the window.

He was deep in thought or no thought and did not move as I climbed into the lower bunk, tried to relax until evening fruit and tea. Oh boy.

As I said, Son was an old pro. He had been meditating daily for about 5 years and had come to the retreat in hopes of finding his dreamed path to perfection, a term which he tried but could not quite describe. I guess that was why he had been asking Clive so many questions. He was unsure of what perfection was and if found how do you know?

I was very impressed with Son, now my official Co-conspirator and soon to become my mentor.

Son came out of his meditative state, turned and looked down from his bunk at me and said, "Hey, let's go for walk before tea time?"

I quietly replied, "Ok, where to?"

"Outside they have path through woods. We walk. You ready."

"Sure, let me get my flip flops."

I stood up, my legs still feeling limp as I got my flips. We walked down a small hallway into the great wide open.

We walked toward the path opening to the woods and slowly moved in silence as we enjoyed the last of the sun bursting through the pines. We maintained our silence, finished our walk just as the gong was sounding the call for fruit and tea, our supper.

Son looked at me and said, "What your name?"

I stammered and said, "Rike, Rike Wilkerson. And you're Son Tranh right?"

"Yep," Son said. "Now we be friends always." He reached out and we shook hands.

I felt a strange shiver as I said, "Yes."

We walked to the dining area and separated as I got some green tea with honey. A large bowl loaded with all types of fruit was placed in the middle of the long wooden table. I picked a banana, a pear and a peach. By this time of day, I was starving.

Getting used to the dining area was another unique experience. You sat next to people you didn't know and couldn't speak with. You ate, then discarded anything you didn't eat into a small compost pot, plates stacked, utensils into a pan.

Then outside with my honey laced tea to watch the final sunset with my new mentor. We enjoyed the quiet of the evening as the setting sun lit the Georgia pines with a blaze that finished the day with twilight of calm.

After supper would be the final sit of each day. During the evening, sit (as it was called) the professional and volunteer staff would join for meditation and discourse. Discourse consisted of an hour lecture on meditation and its history.

It was also a time to relax, meaning you could break your posture and lie back on your cushion and move around without being admonished by the teacher.

During these times, I had caught glimpses of Clive sitting ramrod straight during the meditation hour, listening to the discourse in what looked like a state of rapture. He was, without doubt, truly dedicated. I was curious how someone like Clive came to meditation and how he ended up at the Zen center.

He looked more like a guy you would see at a red neck bar or riding a chopper at Daytona Bike week. I have met many a serious intelligent man who loved his 'bike' but not many who were into Buddhism and meditation. But one should never judge another human until you have walked in their path.

And Clive's life path had included more than a few ups and downs.

During just a few days at the center, Son somehow got the low down on Clive's background and how after years of hard living, he had ended up at the meditation center.

Son told me that Clive had come to the Center after serving time in the Alabama State Pen. Locked up for aggravated assault with a deadly weapon. A rather large knife to be exact. According to Son, the incident that got Clive jail time was a biker bar fight.

Apparently, the aggravation was about Clive's girlfriend, Melanie.

Other bikers standing at the joints bar had been flirting with her. Son said the Clive didn't think it was a big deal. Just typical biker dudes having a few beers and joking with a good-looking woman.

But Clive saw one of the guys slip his hand down the back of Mel's jeans, grabbing her ass, and then things changed for the worse. The point of pissed offense had been Melanie's reaction. She just stood laughing with everyone as the guy eagerly squeezed each butt cheek with a big smile on his face.

Clive standing at the bar watching all this unfold threw some angry words, which grew to Clive's knife and minor but numerous stab wounds to the squeezer. Clive didn't kill him, although that was his intent.

The bartender called the sheriff. Charges were filed, a bum lawyer assigned to the aggravated assault case that was promptly lost and Clive was off to the slammer.

Yet here he was, three years later, meditating in the woods of the deep South.

Weird, but then I thought to myself, *What the hell wasn't weird these days and of course how the hell did Son find all of this out in just a couple of days.*

Questioning and weirdness were the reasons I had come to the meditation center in the first place. I hoped to clear my head of the monstrous craziness that seemed to be washing the human race quickly down the toilet.

At this point, I felt as lost as Clive had probably felt in prison. But lucky for me no bike, no crazy woman, no big knife and no slammer time.

Son also found out that the Zen meditation program had an outreach program for convicts at the prison where Clive had been incarcerated. He had been a good inmate. He strictly followed the rules and stayed on the good side of the guards.

Fortunately, he became involved in meditation. He became a serious and dedicated follower of the teaching, and after only six months became an assistant teacher. He worked hard, stayed clean and was released early for good behavior.

He reunited with Melanie. She begged forgiveness and supposedly had walked a straight path while Clive did his time. After his release from the Alabama Penitentiary, Clive decided their future was Zen meditation and convinced Mel to move to the Zen Center in Georgia.

Now Mel wasn't into the 'meditation thing' as she put it but she was trying her best to stay with Clive and make a go of their life.

First, Clive became an active meditation center volunteer and soon after a full-time staff person. His pay wasn't much but Melanie got a job as a waitress at Lil Rebs Country Cooking restaurant in the small town about three miles from the center.

Each morning, Mel would either ride her Harley sportster to town or catch a ride from one of the other girls she worked with. The tips were good. Mel was cute and the good old boys liked to flirt as she leaned over to clean the tables.

The restaurant was the most popular in the county and was generally packed with hungry folk who tipped pretty well. I have to confess, I ate there once and the so-called country cooking was a far cry from my grandmother's country dinners. I never finished eating the restaurants so called country cooking.

Leaving my plate on the table, I paid up, disillusioned and left leaving a nice tip for Mel.

I only saw Mel a couple of times at the center. Usually in the evening, during our break time, she would come by and meet Clive at the main office. They would walk hand in hand toward their little shotgun house about half mile toward town.

I thought it was nice. But really, what the hell did I know.

Son and I walked through the woods at least once a day during our ten-day sabbatical. Some days, I walked alone just to help clear my head of 'monkey mind' thoughts.

I can't recall exactly when but Son began telling me about various people at the retreat and his keen sense of personalities stimulated my curiosity and voyeuristic instincts.

He spoke quietly about the instructors and the old students and their personal lives. But still this left me confused and wondering, where this was all going. I was more curious than calm, and although, I liked Son, I could not figure out how he learned so much about these people in just a few days.

I was now so confused with all his gossip and the supposed idea of Noble Silence that a sense of apprehension caused me to think about what this guy Son was really about.

The sound of the gong calling for the final sitting of the day startled me as I relaxed against a magnificent oak tree. I abruptly looked up at Son who was staring at me with a friendly smile. He reached and grabbed my hand helping me to my feet.

We walked in silence to the meditation center where we took off our sandals or flops. A large cardboard box at the entry to the meditation hall was full of blankets or ponchos that could be worn during sittings. The nights were pretty cold. It was January.

So I rummaged through the box and found an interesting poncho made from a dark green army blanket with a hole cut out for your head. I thought well that's cool. I wore it day and night for the rest of my stay.

The first few days had come and gone without incident, other than Son telling me about Clive and Mel. He never told me the source of his information. I asked but Son said, "Secret. I know plenty things. People like to tell me because I Vietnamese, and they know we keep secrets until we need not to."

That was confusing. But I didn't bring the subject up again during our private walks.

The last sitting of each day went by quickly as I became more acclimated to the ways of meditation. The lecture, chanting was very calming and relaxing. Afterward, I would take a quick shower, brush my teeth and I was ready for bed.

An old student walked the courtyard ringing the gong for lights out. Son leaned over from his top bunk and say, "Rike, I wake you in morning if you need. Goodnight, good friend."

My first few days in a new world. And for Son and I, Noble Silence became Noble whisper.

Breakfast became a pain. I immediately skipped the usual gray oatmeal that seems to appear at any lengthy camp meeting. Instead, I toasted Ezekiel bread, added organic peanut butter, banana, sun flour seeds and raisin sandwich for breakfast. After the meager evening tea and fruit, the morning breakfast would find me ravenous.

I had to become more creative or the growls of my stomach during meditation sittings, which were distinct, would cause more than a few chuckles.

My newfound breakfast sandwich soon became the favorite of just about everyone. We weren't allowed to speak but you could still see. And those that saw watched as I made and ravenously ate my concoction.

After the sandwich experiment, everyone seemed to ignore the huge pot gray oatmeal and opted for the Rike sandwich which Son called my recipe.

I was proud. I made what I considered to be a positive influence on my fellow meditating travelers.

All was good in Wilkerson world.

I began eating all my meals outside of the main food hall. Son always by my side or sitting across from me smiling. The cool mornings were quite enjoyable. We ate and watched the sun rise.

It slowly warmed us with a new day. Dinner (or lunch) was typically loads of salad and the vegetarian delight of lentil soup. Our evening supper of honey flavored tea and fresh fruit was enjoyed while sitting outside awaiting the sunset. This part of my meditating experience is one I will always remember.

During my ten-day experience, I ate a total of three meals indoors. All others were outside rain or shine. That part of Zen I really loved!

It became apparent from the very first day that I had a real character for a roommate. Son started whispering questions about everything from 'Should I turn out light?' to 'Where you from?' So I joined in and spoke a word or two, thinking that we would both straighten up the next day.

But the talking got worse. We weren't that bad but we sure as hell weren't abiding by the code.

However, when it came to meditation, Son was simply incredible. I had never seen or met anyone so dedicated to his inner peace while sitting. We weren't required to make the first voluntary sitting at 4:30am, but Son never missed and consequently, neither did I.

I grew to love the early morning walk to the meditation building, entering the dimly lit room and sitting on my cushion with my poncho wrapped keeping me warm. I would drift into a quiet slumber and my mind would slowly bend to nothingness.

I began a regimen of half hour of meditation at voluntary sitting, then I would go for a walk on the path through the woods. Then back to our room, shower, change clothes and rest before my restorative breakfast sandwich.

Complex things become simple when you are in a state of solitude. You slow down and concentrate on every movement you make. My sandwich became an important slow motion beginning of each day.

I continued to eat breakfast every morning with Son after which we would walk the path before the first required group sitting at 7am. By 7am, we had been awake 3 hours. So the walks were a good time to stretch and listen to mother nature awake.

However, during these walks Son sometimes talked a bit too much for my solitary soul. He would laugh and tell stories of his life but after a few days, he began telling me more about the center's gossip. I never figured out how he learned this stuff.

Later during the week of our ten-day retreat, I saw him walking with some of the older students. Those that had been to the center before were somehow different. Normally reserved yet with Son, they laughed and joked like school kids.

All the talking and laughing occurred deep in the woods where they couldn't be heard. The older students were those that were supposed to seriously honor Noble silence. Well so much for that stuff!

These dudes were yucking it up, and Son was assuredly in control and in his element. I have to admit; I did get a big kick out of his antics.

It was during our morning walks that Son again began to talk about Clive. I found his knowledge about what was going on behind the scene at the center quite interesting and somehow disturbing. I mean how did my roommate, who could speak only broken English, come to know so much about all of these people so quickly?

But I began participating in the antics of the older student group who met in the backwoods of the center during meditation walks and the gossip flowed. I listened and learned.

Clive was considered by all to be somewhat volatile. His buttons could be easily pushed even after years of dedicated meditation. I happened to notice his anger one morning when I awoke before the ringing of the ceremonial gong.

There were several gongs used at the center. Three were hand held, carried about by old students and struck with a large mallet to awake or announce group meditation and one very large heavy brass gong shaped in the pattern of some type of eastern temple hung on a piece of rope by the kitchen.

Clive was assigned to the kitchen gong to announce 'feeding time'.

Early one morning, I watched from the window in our room as Clive smashed the hell out of the gong with the mallet. He hit it so hard, it broke the rope and sent the 20-pound piece of metal flying across the yard. He was pissed about something; something big.

He quickly ran and picked it up and tied it back to the wood frame of the porch before anyone saw what had happened. But his ruse had not worked. Several volunteers had seen the incident and began to tease Clive.

The teasing was supposedly all in good fun but something struck a taught string in Clive's being. He wasn't upset, he was really pissed off and stayed in that mood for several days.

The fourth day I was called by the teacher to approach and kneel in respect. He told me I had been selected to sit in my own private cell for the full afternoon session. I looked at him dumbfounded.

I nodded my head yes when he asked if I was ready for the meditation time in the cell. That's what they called it the 'meditation cell'.

I was escorted to a door, one of many along a corridor off to the side of the meditation seating. I passed through the door in to a well-lit room with two cushions on the floor. I sat down. The door closed and I was alone. No sound, one clerestory window. And me.

I sat in silence and tried to free my mind of anxiety. No use. I stood up and tried to exercise. I sat and meditated again. I counted backward from 500. I suffered swirls of anxiety. I thought of my friends and relatives that had died.

I said the Lord's prayer over and over and finally remitted and then finally the door opened, my time was up. I walked into the meeting room and as instructed, I approached the teacher and knelt before him. His question to me was simple, "Did you find your inner fears and conquer them?"

I looked at him with tears in my eyes. I bowed my head and said, "Yes, I have seen my soul and know where it must lead me."

"Good," he replied. "Now depart and free your spirit from the corrosive ways of your monkey mind. You may leave your troubled past and walk with the spirit of compassion."

I was limp with mental exhaustion. I walked outside and breathed deeply the fragrant pines of Georgia.

Son was waiting for me. He whispered, "Let us walk. I have interesting story for you that will replace the confusion you are now feeling." Somehow he knew exactly how I felt. My mentor was my strength.

We walked into the woods along the path of 'A thousand steps'. A name I had come up with after counting the steps along the 'path of truth', a name Son had dreamed up.

We walked in silence until we reached the farthest point on the path. Another new student had decided to make some sort of artistic piece on a vacant half-acre of land. It was composed of stone and logs with a Native American TP or tent covered with brush in the middle of the field where he sat.

Son said, "Don't worry about him, he's on a different level. Let's talk gossip."

Son began telling me that Clive was having a tough time with his girlfriend, Melanie. Son said, "She seeing other guys." I said you mean someone else in the Ashram or the town and he said, "No, lots a someone's everywhere," and laughed crazily. This had all occurred within four days at the center.

I am thinking this is bullshit. I'm in the cell losing my way and yet somehow, Son gathered so much information so quickly. However, as I've said many times, his intuition and instincts never ceased to fascinate me.

He had the ability to determine personality traits and make an accurate assessment as to what would happen next after first meeting a person.

During our morning and evening walks, he would frequently stop, hold out his arm for me to stop and then say, "I smell animal." At first, I thought it was a joke. But he would repeat himself, kneel down and smell the grass or bushes next to the walking path.

"I asked what kind of animal?"

He replied, "Big animal, maybe deer, maybe coyote."

I said jokingly, "Maybe just a squirrel."

And Son replied, "No big animal."

I shrugged these occurrences off until the fourth day when he said, "I smell animal," and I looked off to the side and there was a dog or coyote looking animal eating voraciously on the body of a fawn deer. The hungry animal looked at us with glaring eyes then went back to the fawn.

Son gently touched my arm and whispered, "Don't move, danger." The animal began dragging the dead fawn into the deeper part of the woods. Son signaled that we should keep walking. Admittedly, I was very scared. I had never seen something so striking, yet amazing.

After we walked a while in silence, Son started to laugh and said, "I told you I smell animal, I know these things."

"What was that thing eating the fawn?" I stammered.

Son looked straight in the eye. "That thing is cayo dog."

"A what?" I asked.

"It's how you say? Cross between dog and coyote. Very dangerous. We lucky it not attack us. That why I say don't move. They very dangerous because they not afraid of people like dog and very mean as coyote can be."

"I only seen few. We be careful in these woods. They can kill you."

So, what has this got to do with Clive? Son made me realize that he really had some instinct as to what was occurring in and around him. An intuitive recognition of life. He could smell, touch, feel and enjoy the humor and danger, so it seemed, of all existence.

These brief episodes had a dramatic impact on me. But more, much more was to come.

I spoke earlier of day 2 and the difficulties the teacher had warned we might encounter. The teachers were correct.

Day 2 of meditation was for me a nightmare of mind wandering, incredible daydreams, horrible flashbacks and unending panic attacks. Day 4 in the cell was tough, but day 2 was frightful. I thought of the brutality that prisoners of war were put through.

My small trial in the cell was nothing compared to their experience but for me, day 2 was as close to insanity as I wanted to get. Day 1, your mind was adjusting to a mild environment where everything was new and easy going.

Day 2, the mind wandered. Thoughts of every sin, every, miscalculation made in a relationship, everything you'd made in life then lost.

The supposed poor parent you had become, 'where is this all going', and on and on for hours. Son's only comment after the 2nd day of meditation had been, "Boy that be bad freaking day"

Jeez, I really liked this guy. Straight at 'em and could smell where a deer had crossed and the crazy cayo dog. What was next? Of course it had to be something about Clive…the guy who wanted perfection who had tried to explain how to achieve total immersion into life and ask for nothing to a person who was at peace but seeking more. And that of course was Son.

Moving on to day 5, Clive seemed more restless in the dining area and in meditation. He was very distressed and had to leave meditation several times. His concentration was gone. He wandered aimlessly around the center and Mel hadn't been seen in two days.

Son said during our morning walk, "Clive smell bad, he smell like blood." I was taken aback.

"You mean animal blood?"

Son said, "No, human blood." Well that scared the hell out of me. I asked did he hurt someone? Son said, "Maybe but more be coming."

Day 5 came and went quietly as I had become accustomed to the routine of eating, sleeping and meditating. I finally had relaxed. Time in the cell had knocked the wind out of my ego.

Meditation and other students became familiar and somehow silently supporting. Their efforts at meditative practice were actually very inspirational.

Day 6 started as usual with the first sittings then walks then eat then sit. But dinner was a topper. The men's group had all silently filed into the eating area where the food was already on the large serving table. Clive usually handled the chore of bringing more food, tea or water as needed.

Son and I both made huge salads and bowls of lentil soup which hunger had driven me to like. We took our food and went outside to eat and enjoy the noonday sun.

Suddenly, there was loud shouting and screaming coming from inside the dining hall. I quickly turned to see what caused the commotion when the screen door opened and the ashram head master came running with his head bleeding profusely and his right-hand gushing blood from where three of his fingers used to be.

Then Clive literally ran through the screen door with a huge kitchen knife in his hand yelling, "You mother fucker, you're going to die." We all sat dumbfounded. I saw Son jump at Clive and with a quick sweep of his feet, Clive collapsed and Son gave him a hand chop to the throat leaving Clive desperately gasping for air.

Some in the group jumped on Clive and held him down while I ran after the head master who was running down the road screaming. I finally caught up with him and ripped off my T-shirt and wrapped his bleeding hand. The cut on his forehead was superficial but the hand was a mess.

Someone called 911 and the sheriff and Meds showed up in about 15 minutes.

I thought, *Well so much for dinner and Noble silence.* Everyone was chattering away; questions were asked. Clive got into the sheriff's car quietly with his hands cuffed behind him. The head master went away in the ambulance. The rest of us stood and looked as dumbfounded as we felt.

The teachers were right. Day 6 was tough. We all went to the walking trail and in the back of the wooded area the gossip began.

Son had been right. The smell of blood was right on. Clive had confronted Mel about the rumors that were circulating through town and the center. An argument led to a serious fight, which led to Clive stabbing Melanie to death in their little house. Always a knife deal with this whacked out dude.

Then he went after the first guy on his 'to do' list which was the head master. Apparently, the head master and Mel had been involved in a red neck swingers club. Yep, they do exist. So Clive wanted revenge and he knew whom he would make pay for this humiliation and disgust that overcame him.

The head master had lost two fingers; one was successfully sewed back on. Son had saved his life.

We struggled on with our meditations after a lengthy group discussion about the so-called incident. We all made it through until day 10. I actually got back into my routine, although Clive's empty cushions were a constant reminder of that crazy 6th day.

After day 10, we were allowed to openly speak. Introductions and discussions about the craziness we all experienced and then it was over.

And then we all parted ways.

Son went back home to his business in Atlanta. I left early in the morning and stopped at McDonald's for coffee and an egg and sausage McMuffin. So much for vegetarianism.

Sadly, Clive went back to prison. He would be gone for a long time. I heard later that he was teaching meditation this time at the Georgia State prison.

The Zen meditation center is still going and growing. I am frequently asked would I go back? Yeah I really liked it. Do I stay in touch with Son? Yep, talked to him this morning. He wished me happy blessings and said, "Good friend, you will have good year."

I Believe Him

TIN CAN

It had taken me all day to get the damn trailer straightened up.

I had worked myself into frenzy and needed a straight out of the bottle dose of medication. The half empty gallon bottle of vodka was handy, so I worked on it until I was semi-conscious. But I plowed on with the work that needed attention.

Now to see if my handiwork had been noticed by any of the other misbegotten sons a bitch in this trailer heaven dump I called home.

I carefully pushed the front door open and peaked out at another sweat worthy Texas summer day. The trailer park was quiet. I pushed the door wide open and took my first step on the rickety trailer stairs, feeling the full blast from the scorching Texas sun.

I took a long leisurely innocent looking stretch and casually glanced up and down the trailer lined street.

Not a soul. Not a car moving. Not a dog or cat in sight. Nothing. Just the silent motion of heat waves pealing up from the spongy hot asphalt street.

Damn, I felt lucky. Apparently, no one heard all the previous night's commotion and called the cops. Maybe I was ok? But then again maybe was a dangerous word when you've just killed someone.

I thought, *How the hell was I going to get myself out of this damn mess?*

I had left work early the day before and decided to head straight home. The same old beginning of every pathetic story about your woman and some other guy.

Nothing new in life, just my turn to suffer.

I had called it a day because nothing was selling at my used car lot.

Used cars were my trade and if you happen to be one of those that don't respect a hard workingman, then you can stick it. I had busted my ass to get a little business going, and all the response I got from folks was 'You're what?' A used car salesman!

Yep, so what the hell? I worked hard and was damn proud of what I'd accomplished so far in my so-called life.

Standing in the heat every day, sweat pouring off me by the gallon as I tried to sell some poor Mexican or broke down white dude a piece of crap I had just bought at the auto auction. Yeah, that's usually how it all works for the poor sap trying to buy a ride for the family or to get to his job. Bad credit? No problem, I'd tote the note.

Knowing full well that I'd probably re-po the car and around and around the game would go. But I did what I could to keep it all together and hopefully, give the buyer some kind of break. Usually, it all went haywire and I'd start over again. Same car, new rube.

My main man and spot on genius mechanic, Juan, would get the car running good, at least good enough to get it off the lot. The car would usually last six or nine months. As I said, I'd hold the paper at a reasonable but profitable 16% interest rate. Most of my buyers dicn't have credit good enough to buy a lawn mower, much less a car. But I did my best to at least get 'em a ride.

Then after the poor guy or gal quit paying because the car broke down or more likely just quit running, Then Juan's brother, Jesus, would pay a visit, load up the car bring it back to the sales lot and the roller coaster ride would start again. Typical everyday work in the cheap used car business.

Year in and year out just plain boring stuff that at least paid my bills. Without a doubt though, Jesus had the toughest job. Constantly hammering poor people for money when their luck had finally given out.

When Jesus showed up, it was pay up or he'd hitch the car to his truck, drive off and ignore the part time owners yelling and cursing. Tough job but Jesus loved it. 'Nailing them' is what he called it. Weird.

Sticking it to folks and calling it a legal living was somewhat of a stretch. But what the hell was I supposed to do? I figured I'd bust my ass and after I made some extra dinero I'd move up to the bigger leagues and sell some decent stuff.

But then I got a little side tracked on my big life adventure. Yeah sure dope, booze, wild and crazy women had been major obstacles on the road to my eventual success. But I knew I had the huevos to pull myself out of the ditch and get into the big time.

Then, I met Tina and it went from great to terrible mighty damn quick.

It had been a tough week with no sales. So on Tuesday, I locked the doors and headed out. Told Juan and Jesus adios and to take the rest of the day off.

I thought I'd do some chores around the trailer and keep the little woman happy. I left the car lot and stopped at Harry's liquor for a half gallon of Popov vodka for a little inspiration and got home just in time to see Dennis, my best friend, leaving my trailer. He drove right by me and gave a friendly wave as my 69 Camaro rumbled down the street past him.

Funny, he waved but didn't stop to talk. I figured he had work or something else on his mind.

I turned into my driveway got out and walked up the damn trailer stairs and opened the door. There stood my little beauty Tina, wearing high cut short shorts and a wife beater T-shirt and no bra.

"Hey, darlin," she said and I broke into a needless sweat. She was such a cutie. But then aren't they all cute when scantily dressed and looking like sex gone wild.

Hell yes, at that moment I was crazy for her.

Then she said, "So you want a drink after a tough day?"

"Of course, and make yourself one too. We can party down."

She got a tray of ice out of the frig and cracked it open in the sink. Dropping a couple of cubes into the glasses as I said, "Now don't be shy make us both a double."

With the drinks poured from the big jug of Popov, we sat back on my yellow plaid mobile-home couch and flipped on the tube.

She was such a screamer. It didn't take much time till my pants were around my boots and she was working on me as hard as she could.

I wasn't about to say slow down. So soon I had her jacked up on the couch and was ready to lay it on.

In the course of so-called foreplay, things just didn't seem quite right. She had a strange musky tint as if she had been playing with fire earlier without me.

I thought to myself, *Hell someone's been here before me! This is too smooth and easy going.* I'd felt that way before and thought well she's just hot to trot. But now I began to wonder if maybe Dennis had been checking out my personal territory.

His casual little wave as he drove by and the lip-synched 'Hey dude' through his closed car window. That was a little too casual for good buddies.

That was my crazy little thought? But what the hell I might as well wail away and have my fun till I find out for sure if someone had been mischievously loving on my crazy, darling little wife.

This little escapade went on for a while. Me trying to figure out the schedule of events and who exactly was trespassing on my territory. The more I thought and figured, the more pissed off I became. It had to be Dennis.

But Dennis had been a longtime friend. All the way back to Alamo Heights High in San Antonio where we had been not just great friends but like really solid buds.

But time had passed and slowly with each year we all got older and drifted on with our separate lives.

But poor Dennis just got a little older and a bit faster than the rest of my friends. Doing crack with wild women and holding a job just wasn't in the hand he played. Especially, if one of the wild women just might be your best friend's wife.

After several mistaken laden attempts at college and random military assignments before, he was booted out of the Army, Dennis had found himself sitting alone in a tin box in the country outside of Bandera wondering, what the hell just happened? He never understood that when you're sitting at the table and don't know who the mullet is, you're it.

He finally got a steady job selling water softeners. Made nothing to speak of but enough that kept him in cigarettes and gin. Boy always loved them Tini's as he called them. Hmmm, now there's a coincidence. Tini and Tina.

Me? I was always good with cars, so career wise I naturally drifted that way.

Dennis finally found his calling in life. He could talk through about anything and sell anyone some lousy water softener or whatever else he was selling that month. He became that kind of guy. Great talker but never could take advantage of a good break.

He always screwed something up. Usually crack cocaine was involved as he stumbled along through life, hanging on by any thread he could grasp.

Yet, Dennis and I seemed to be cool, so I thought, and that was that.

A few weeks went by and then another slow day. I locked up and decided to stop in at Mary's, the local alcoholic drinking joint.

Mary had been a big ol gal but had been dead for about four years. Early heart attack. But her joint still served big drinks cheap and offered all customers a never-ending cloud of cigarette smoke. The place reeked of booze. The floors old red carpet probably had a case of vodka soaked into its well-worn fibers.

I pounded a few drinks down paid the tab, stepped out into the swelter they call August in Texas and headed for my tin can home.

As I turned into the trailer park, Green Acres, what a name, I saw Dennis' car parked in front of my trailer. No coincidence this time. I parked down the street and walked behind the neighbors and quietly walked to the back door of my trailer.

I reached up but the door was locked. I figured I would make a full frontal military style assault. So I eased up the trailers rickety steps, carefully put my key into the door and opened it slowly. I saw no one. The stereo was on but nothing in the living room.

Then I heard some shuffling in the back bedroom and heard the back or side door of the trailer swing open. I quickly opened the front door and watched as Dennis jump out the door and running with his shirttail flapping heading for his car. "Goddamn you," was all I could come up with.

Then I hollered, "Tina," and ran back toward the bedroom. And there she stood buck naked, standing in the corner.

"What the fuck are you doing?" I said. She stood completely still. Not a move, not a word, nothing but a slight smirk and crooked smile.

But then she made her big mistake. "What's it look like?" She said in a smart-ass way that royally pissed me off.

"I'll tell you what it looks like, it looks like you and Dennis have been screwing your brains out. And for some time now?"

Seething with anger at being caught, she yelled, "Well so what? I like him. And he's a better lay than you are. Maybe twice as good. Maybe three times as good! So there. You don't like it, get the hell out!"

"Why, you crazy little slut," I hissed. "This is my place not yours, and if there's any getting out it will be your sorry little ass. In fact, I'm throwing you out right now. Out the same back door that lousy bastard Dennis went out."

Her nasty reply was the final jolt to my jealous rage. "You don't have the balls to do anything like that, you dumb used car shit."

Now let's take a little break here. I didn't know where all this was coming from. I had taken her from a broke down dumpy little town in north Texas, brought her to San Antonio and helped her get a new life. And now she was throwing this no count prick of a friend in my face as super stud-boy.

"Why I oughta knock the hell out of you."

"Just try it," she snarled. "You don't have the balls to do dick. Which is why I've fucked every man, including Dennis, since you can't seem to keep your little spark plug lit up enough to do me any favors."

That did it. I hauled back and hit her square in the face. I mean right on the nose. I heard the cartilage crack and man did my heart jump! Maybe I can't go at it as hard as others but I'm not gonna let some redneck slut question my manhood. So I socked her again in the temple for good measure.

She fell back on the bed with a floppy sounding thud. Nose bleeding like hell all over her naked body. She lay there moaning.

Then she muttered through her blood soaked mouth, "You impotent drunk bastard. I'll get you for this."

That's when I really lost it. Beside the bed on the nightstand was her pink hairdryer. I picked it up and held it by the blower end and began bashing her face and head.

She tried to yell but I put my hand over her mouth and kept smashing away. Those little plastic dryers are pretty durable. It never broke. So I kept pounding her head and face until she didn't move.

I held my hand tightly over her nose and mouth and squeezed her throat until she stopped breathing. As I released my handgrip on her neck, a little bubble of breath tinged in red came from her mouth. She was done.

I left the room leaving her on the bed and went to the kitchen of the damn trailer and got a tea glass filled in to the brim with Popov and drank it down like water.

Christ, what was I going to do now.

It was then that I opened the door of my tin can to see if anyone in the surrounding trailers had heard or seen anything. Not a soul in sight. Nothing but the sound of air conditioners hanging from windows whirring away. I turned on the phones answering machine making sure to record any inquiring calls for Tina.

Then nonchalantly walked to my car and headed straight to Mary's.

I drove to Mary's parked in near the front door so I could be seen the other serious drinkers. As I got out of the car, I checked myself for bloodstains, then casually entered and eased up to the end of the bar and ordered a double Jack and coke.

As Branch, the bartender, pored my drink, I asked if he had the time. He pointed to the clock under the deer head stuck on the wall and said, "About 5:30. Looks like you're right on time, Chance."

Yeah that's the name my old man gave me. He thought it was unique and was always saying, "Give Chance a chance and he'll do just about anything." I guess he was right. Here I was having a drink while my little Tina was in the bed, dead.

I thought, *Oh well what's done is done and 5:30 gives me a fairly tight alibi.* At least, for now.

I had to figure out how the hell was I going to get rid of Tina? I was pretty damn shaken up.

I called to Branch. "Gimme another double. I got to go home and tell the old lady it was another shit day at the car lot."

"Gotcha covered, bubba. You want something to munch on before you split? Don't want you filling your gut with too much Jack and no food."

"Yeah sure, slide those pickled eggs my way and let me have a burger and fries. I haven't eaten all day." It was around 9:30 when I left.

I had shifted from Jack and coke to Lone Star beer to slow my drinking and stay reasonably levelheaded.

During my heavy thinking at Mary's, I came up with a simple but potentially good plan. A real jewel of a serious screwing for Dennis if there ever was one.

Dennis had bought his hunk of junk car from me about two months ago and I still had a matching set of keys. I figured I would haul Tina's little ass out the door of my trailer to my car. Take her to Dennis's car. Dump her in the back seat and see what happened next.

Serve the shithead right. Banging my woman all the time and hopping out the backdoor when I came home. I mean who wouldn't be pissed.

An old Texas rule, you don't screw your best friend's woman ever. Much less expect to get away with it.

I left Mary's drove home and pulled quietly into my driveway with the headlights and the motor turned off. I eased the car door open and carefully pushed it closed. I unlocked the trunk.

Then walked carefully up the steps, opened the front door and made my way to the back of the trailer. I turned the side light on the table next to the bed and there she was naked with her face covered in blood. Not a lot of blood elsewhere but her face was pretty damn beat up.

She hadn't moved, but the little slut was sure enough dead. She pushed too hard and had it coming. I checked the answering machine and luckily, no calls. Things were looking up.

I rolled Tina up in the sheets and bed cover and carefully checked for any sign of bloodstains. No sign of any struggle. No other lights on in the trailer.

I eased my way to the front careful not to touch anything with the sheet and bed cover tightly wrapped around the body of my little darlin. Bitch.

I looked through the curtains covering the living room window checking the trailer park out real good. I sure didn't need any eyes peeping. There were just a few dim lights on in the neighborhood. I thought 'all clear' as I carefully walked down the stairs and quietly as possible loaded her body in the trunk of the car.

I looked around at the other tin cans in the neighborhood. All the lights were now off. I made sure to bring the pink hair dryer and her panties, which I later dropped in a dumpster behind an icehouse where I stopped to pick up a 6 pack of lone star and a bag of pork skins. Hard work makes a man thirsty and hungry.

After I had slammed a few beers, I began to feel a little lonely. I mean, man, I was really crazy about Tina. Had been since I first saw her at Mary's. Jeez thinking about her in the trunk made me feel kind of sad.

Well not that sad and definitely not lonely. The little bitch had played too hard on my dime and now she would give Dennis the final real hard screwing for the last time. By the time he got out of the slammer, he would be as numb as he was dumb.

Dip shit son of bitch. Serve him right. Just thinking about him jumping out of that damn trailer drove me nuts.

I damn near rear-ended the car in front of me as my brain went all jealous on me. Now that would surely have been a headline on the local blood and guts news TV station.

Around 2am, I pulled into Dennis' apartment building parking area and found a convenient vacant parking space next to his car. He lived in a dump section 8 project, just off loop 410 near Helotes Valley. Broke down folks, as well as hard working Mexicans were his neighbors.

All crashed out after a tough day trying to make a decent living for their families. A hard life.

But more importantly, not a soul in sight. No lights on and luckily, Dennis's car parked out of sight beside the apartments trash dumpster. My luck was running hot.

I eased out of my car, quietly walked to Dennis's car, unlocked and opened the back door. I then carefully removed Tina from the trunk of my car and put her into Dennis's backseat. I unrolled the sheets and blanket and her body rolled to the floor in the backseat with a thump.

She was all wiggly looking like a busted doll. My little busted naked doll with her cute ass popping up in the air. But the ugly memories came back as I quickly covered the body with the blanket and sheets from the bed where they'd been going at it. I figured Dennis's DNA would be all over the damn thing and especially all over Tina.

I wiped everything in and on Dennis' car carefully with a clean rag, closed the door as quietly as I could and carefully wiped the door handle clean. I figured any other prints or DNA from me could easily be justified since I had previously owned the damn car and had slept on the sheets.

I took off my t-shirt and jeans and on the way back to tin can city, threw everything I had touched in a big dumpster next to a new office building under construction.

Things were looking better in my neighborhood. New buildings going up everywhere, shopping centers. All signs of a fast-growing city. Too bad Dennis wouldn't be around to see how much nicer things would be in ten to fifteen years or more. I chuckled as I thought well he'd get enough ass in Huntsville and vice versa. More vice then versa I would expect.

I figured I had done all I could to cover my tracks. Drove home in my underwear and decided I better check the tin can out for any blood stains or anything that might connect me with the crime scene. I wiped a few places with some diluted vinegar that Tina used to clean with and that was that.

Put clean sheets on the bed and laid down for a few hours' sleep. Now all I needed to do was wait it out. I knew the cops would be calling sooner rather than later.

Next morning, I woke up around 8 and watched the news. Nothing yet. I made coffee, cleaned up some more and walked out to pick up my paper. Saw my neighbor, Julie, two tin boxes down the street. Waved and said, "Mornin', Julie, feels like another hot day is headed our way."

"Yep, how you and Tina taking this heat?"

"Not too bad, whenever she's home."

Julie looked at me and smiled. "You two getting along ok over there?"

"I think so," I said looking down at my flip-flops. "Why'd ya ask?"

Julie slyly replied, "Oh I seen another bee crusin' around here buzzing at your hive."

Acting quite startled I said, "Ya gotta be kidding me, what'd the car look like?"

"Like the one your friend Denney drives, and I see it stop for a good while now and then."

"Well, maybe that explains where Tina's gotten off to. Damn women. Oh, I'm sorry, Julie, I meant damn woman."

"Nah, I understand. Some women just can't get enough pecker."

"Ah now your pushing my manhood," I said jokingly.

"Well, you ever want a cold beer on a hot day just come on over and talk to Ms. Julie about the world of women."

"I just might do that; you still on the divorce circuit?"

"Yeah but staying home is really getting boring as hell."

"Well, I think Tina and I will get things worked out. Gal's crazy about me."

"Right," Julie said sarcastically. "When you've had enough, let me know. Say hi to Tina," she turned to pick up her paper and that hot little butt poked out through her jean shorts. My poor brain went ahh silently, but still a little moan.

"Tell er when I see er, you take care."

"I always do," she said. "I know what a man likes."

At that, I swallowed hard and walked back into the trailer. Shot of bourbon in the coffee might sooth my nerves. *Jesus Christ,* I thought, *I had just killed Tina and women were already after me.*

An old Texas barroom saying, "Women, you can't live with them and you can't kill 'em." But I had killed Tina and now I needed to straighten up. Get my story down pat.

I guess my old man was right, "Give Chance a chance and he'll do anything."

So later the next day, I was at the car lot, sweating like a 3 balled tomcat on the 4th when two cops rolled up in a black and white. They got out walked over and said, "Hey, Chance, missing anything?"

Smart ass son of a bitch.

"Well, nothing on the lot but I ain't seen my wife in a day or two which is mighty damn strange."

"Well," the cop said slowly as he and his partner walked toward me.

"We got some tough news and some questions for you."

"So I always want the tough news first, what is it? Be glad to have you boys in for some coffee and a doughnut. And whatever it is I'll be glad to help if I can."

The big cop said in a matter-of-fact tone, "Mr. Connery we found your wife dead in the back of a car that you apparently sold to a Mr. Dennis Lang."

"Say what?" I practically shouted.

The cop said again. "We found Tina Connery, your wife, in the backseat of Dennis Lang's car. I'm afraid she's dead."

I choked and my voice broke, as I whimpered, "No, no, no, this can't be happening. Please tell me that this is a mistake of some kind. Denney was always running wild with women but killing one, especially Tina, that just ain't like him."

"Well, he told us he hasn't seen your wife in a couple of days but that doesn't explain the body in his car."

"In his car? What the hell is going on? Is Denney ok?" I said with deep concern.

The big cop replied, "We've got him in custody for interrogation. When was the last time you saw your wife."

I told the cops I'd seen Tina the day before yesterday when I got home from work and all was fine. She was busy fixing something for supper and we watched TV and I crashed. But yesterday, she was gone when I got home.

"Didn't think much about it cause sometimes she'll spend the night at her sister's, especially if they've been out partying."

The lead cop asked his partner, "Did you talk to her sister?"

"Yeah," the other cop replied. "The sister said she hadn't seen her for a week. A neighbor of Mr. Larg's called 911 when they saw him lifting something that looked like a body covered with a blanket from the back seat of his car."

"Jesus Christ," I said, "I can't believe this."

I started to weep and continued to sob as the cop said, "Could you think of any reason Mr. Lang would want to kill your wife?"

"Hell no, everyone liked Tina. Hell, Denney was my best friend. He saw her a lot but there wasn't any foolin' around even when we were all loaded. Denney had more women than he could handle."

"You will need to come with us to answer some questions and identify the body." The cop talked real slow as if he was on to something.

"Oh Jesus, help me. I don't know if I can take all of this so suddenly; can't this wait?" I begged.

"Fraid not," the sly skinny cop said, "we need the ID pronto and a statement from you."

"Are you arresting me or something?" I said with surprise but no fear.

"No, we just need to talk but we will read you your rights and you can follow us downtown to the station to tell us all about your friend, Denney, and your wife."

"Ok," I said. "Let me get my car and I'll be glad to follow. I do know my rights but I'll do anything and answer any questions to get to the bottom of this. I love my wife."

"Well," said the cop, "let me read you what your rights are just for the record."

So he raddled on and I said I understood.

We went out into the heat wave and I hollered at Juan to bring me a car to drive downtown.

"Sure, Boss," and he wheeled around the corner of the lot in my car.

"Let's go, I'll follow you guys to the station," I said to the cops.

Now this is where Juan had come in mighty handy. He had taken the Camaro that Tina had been in and completely detailed it and was ready to put it on the lot for sale. I love Mexican's. They are right up there with Cubans when it comes to smart town.

Never a word spoken. Juan tossed me the keys and said, "You want me to stay here, Boss?"

"Yeah, Juan. You and Jesus take care of things. I'll be back soon. Sell something and I'll bonus you both."

Juan responded, "Si, Jefe. Call me if any problems."

So off we go to the cop station. We got there; I parked in a spot marked for visitors and walked in. They told me to sit and wait. Then out comes Denney in handcuffs walking right by me.

I said, "Denney," looking very concerned, "what the hell is going on?"

Before he could answer, the cop with him said, "You both be quiet, hear me?" I nodded my head yes and was glad the cop shut me up before I said something stupid.

The cops motioned for me to follow them and we went into some small room with a camera on the wall and they told me to sit down and relax, that this would only take a few minutes, which in cop talk means 'until we get you to fess up or we believe your bullshit'.

They started in with the usual good cop bad cop crap. 'Want a smoke, want a coke? Where were you two nights ago, when did you get home, did you stop anywhere on the way home? Did you love your wife? Did you know she was having an affair with your friend, Denney?'

And that's where I went all in on the pretend surprised and deeply offended.

"What the hell are you talking about?" The old reverse trick of putting them on the defense. Like Darrell Royal said 'the best defense is a good offence'.

So I started hammering the hell out of them. "Who told you anything different? Of course I loved my wife. Why would you say something so outrageous to a man who just found out his wife is dead and you haven't even shown me a body?"

"What the fuck do you think I am, Christ, someone killed my wife and you're asking me these stupid cop questions and I don't even know if it's my wife that's dead? Either you guys show me or tell me something or I'm not saying another word without my attorney."

So they stopped dead in their dumbass tracks and realized they had really screwed up. The question hung in the air. Was the dead woman my wife or not?

They tried to reverse course, "Well, your friend identified her."

"You mean to tell me you bring me down here to identify a woman that is supposed to be my wife and before I can see her, you show her to the last person who was apparently with the woman YOU THINK may be my wife! You show her to the guy who just passed me in the hallway in handcuffs? What the fuck is going on with you people?"

This shook their asses up. They knew they had really screwed the pooch on this one.

I knew they had a camera on me so as soon as they both left the room, I let out a moan and started to cry. I'm good at that. Actually, I was thinking about was the time I had to kill my pet calf when my family lived on a ranch in Cotulla. Still hurt to have killed that calf. Man, did I sob.

Finally, dimmy and dimmer came back in, apologized and said, "Let's go see if we have your wife."

So we get in their cop car and go to the local morgue, get out, walk in and talk to some guy in a white coat with a few bloodstains on it then into the refrigerated morgue room.

They wheel out this sheet covered body and tell me to prepare myself and then pull back the sheet. And there she is, my sweet little Tina, all cleaned up except for the big crack in her nose and I burst out in a gag reflex and sobbed, "Yes, yes, that is my beautiful Tina."

The cop asks, "So this is your wife?"

I'm sobbing uncontrollably as I say, "Yes, how did she get like this? Where did you find her?"

I wanted to ask could you roll her over and let me look at her cute little ass one more time? But I didn't want to be that stupid, so I continued to think about my calf and cried till they took her away.

So they let me go after hearing the story about going to Mary's and about talking to Julie and where I was when and how long I'd known Denny, and on and on with more dumbass questions about Tina and Denney.

Later, I found out when they went to Mary's, verified times and what I ate and other cop crap. Then they had gone to my neighbor, Julie's, who told them a whole lot of stuff about Denney jumping out the back door of the trailer, and apparent fights that Denney and Tina had, which I knew nothing about but Julie seemed to know a lot about.

A couple of days later, they dropped by the car lot and talked to Juan who told them about my car and that it had been sold which was typically the way we handled business.

So they had reached a dead end, which left only Denney as the prime suspect.

As expected, his DNA was everywhere even where I had never been, up in her hair, on her tits. Christ the guy was a regular cum machine. So my thoughts of Tina faded off to slut town. She was just another cock-loving bitch in heat.

Denney had no money, so he got a court appointed dumbass lawyer who barely knew where the courthouse was. His lawyer made an absolute mess of everything. Hell when he was finished even I thought Denney had killed her.

Then Julie was called and proved to be an awesome witness. She testified that she thought Denney and Tina had been going at it for some time. They would have frequent screaming matches and fights, with Denney jumping out the back door just as I was walking in the front door.

She'd seen it all. Julie was the best witness I could have wished for.

Julie was a very nice and attractive woman. She lived alone and had a slight disability problem.

Years before I met her, she had been deer hunting with some friends on a ranch in west Texas. One of her inexperienced friends was unloading her rifle after a day in the deer stand and accidently shot Julie's left arm half off.

Luckily for her, she was right-handed but regardless, she was declared disabled and got a monthly check, plus she sued the knucklehead that shot her and got a pretty large settlement from the insurance sharks. Being home alone, she apparently saw lots and lots of weird things going on at my tin can with the rickety front steps and the back door slamming.

God bless her.

Found guilty of second-degree murder, Denney got twenty years at Huntsville with a chance of parole after fifteen. Tough sentence but he had committed a bad crime.

He had been enjoying the sexual impulses of my horny slut of a wife.

Texas law is tough on adultery, particularly when it's the woman who's doing the adultering. The way I figured, they both got what they deserved.

After a few weeks of sulking, Julie asked me to come by for a little wine and a visit. I said sure.

I went over one afternoon and I arrived, she opened the door handed me a glass of wine. I couldn't help but notice she was in a dress so light it revealed no under wear. I mean nada. So I stepped into her trailer and we had a nice glass of wine and puffed on something or other and then got it on.

She was super turned on and fortunately had her right hand working pretty well. We went after it like a couple of coked out porn stars. I fell for her immediately. We would get after it and get after it then talk all night until Mr. Happy could stand no more happiness, and I had fallen madly in love.

And it stayed that way.

About six months later, we decided to get married and get out of trailer park city. She had the money from her insurance and for some reason, I caught a good run selling cars and made some good bucks. Then I was approached by a close friend of Julie's who offered to back me on a small Chrysler dealership in a small town outside of Llano.

He had another dealership and said the Chrysler deal was to small and the company was desperate to sell cars and were damn near giving them away. I thought about it and after talking to Julie, I agreed to give it a go. After all, my name is Chance.

We married, sold our tin joints, pooled the money, found a great little town in the hill country and opened for business. Later, I was lucky and got a Honda motorcycle franchise and things just took off.

Of course there was Denney. I went to see him in Huntsville a couple of times. He looked like shit. Pasty white, dark circles, usually half beaten up. But over time, he toughened up and started to look like a real con. He, of course, found 'the Lord' but never figured out how Tina got whacked. He was always dumb that way.

He could sell good but couldn't buy right.

And my life? It continued on far beyond my wildest expectations.

Julie and I have two kids, live in Mason, Texas in a great house we bought and restored. Got 200 acres. The kids are great and Julie's an unbelievable mother and wonderful wife.

I expanded my business, sold it and somehow ended up with a Mercedes Benz dealership on loop 1604 north of San Antonio. Juan and Jesus stayed with me. Juan is now the sales manager and Jesus is the head service manager. Our dealership became one of the hottest selling Benz dealer in the country.

Life and luck had collided and settled on us all.
I took a chance and never looked back.